ALL THE WRONG PLACES

A CARA WALDEN MYSTERY

ALL THE WRONG PLACES

LISA LIEBERMAN

FIVE STAR
A part of Gale, Cengage Learning

GALE
CENGAGE Learning·

Farmington Hills, Mich • San Francisco • New York • Waterville, Maine
Meriden, Conn • Mason, Ohio • Chicago

GALE
CENGAGE Learning

LIBRARY OF CONGRESS CATALOGING-IN-PUBLICATION DATA

Lieberman, Lisa.
    All the wrong places / Lisa Lieberman. — First edition.
        pages cm. — (A Cara Walden mystery ; 1)
        ISBN 978-1-4328-3023-6 (hardcover) — ISBN 1-4328-3023-6 (hardcover)
        1. Actresses—Fiction. 2. Americans—England—Fiction. 3. London (England)—History—20th century—Fiction. 4. Sicily (Italy)—History—1945—Fiction. 5. Mystery fiction. 6. Love stories. I. Title.
PS3612.I3347A79 2015
813'.6—dc23   2014041371

First Edition. First Printing: March 2015
Find us on Facebook– https://www.facebook.com/FiveStarCengage
Visit our website– http://www.gale.cengage.com/fivestar/
Contact Five Star™ Publishing at FiveStar@cengage.com

Printed in the United States of America
1 2 3 4 5 6 7 19 18 17 16 15

ALL THE WRONG PLACES

CHAPTER ONE:
WALDEN LODGE
HOLLYWOOD, CALIFORNIA,
SUMMER 1941

*I believe that the person you are when you're eight years old
is the person you really are.*

I was creeping up on Geoffrey as he sat meditating on the lawn—not that I could be invisible, my girl's body draped in my mother's mink coat—but Geoffrey was in one of his trances. I could have danced naked in front of him and he'd have continued to stare into the void.

Sometimes I did go naked; lots of people did at Walden Lodge in those days. My father was known as a bohemian and bathing suits were optional around the pool, although you had to dress for dinner in the lodge. Winters could be chilly even in Southern California, but there were always a few diehards who went skinny dipping regardless of the weather. Starlets who'd do anything to get a part in one of Father's pictures. Englishmen, like Geoffrey, who'd gone to boarding schools where they made you bathe in cold water, year-round. He got used to it, found it invigorating. "Manly," as my brother Gray put it, the arch tone in his voice laced with affection.

"Gray, darling. How would you know?" said Vivien, my mother, in the same tone, minus the affection.

I paused to kick off Vivien's high heels, which kept sinking into the earth. Barefoot, I moved stealthily over the silky grass, stalking my prey. The air smelled of citrus, the overripe sweetness of oranges that had fallen on the ground and were beginning to rot in the sun. We picked as many as we could, but there were always fruits we couldn't reach.

Years later, when I was in Sicily filming a B-movie with Adrian, beautiful, wounding Adrian, we stayed in a *pensione* in Taormina. Three months with my love in Italia! The movie was forgettable but I finagled a print from the director, mostly because of my scenes with Adrian. The Italian actress they got to dub my dialogue had this wonderful, husky voice. It's a treat watching us in Italian, where you don't have to pretend to follow the plot.

The *pensione* had a swimming pool set in a terraced garden that reminded me of Father's, complete with lemon trees. For breakfast, they served us juice made from blood oranges. I couldn't get over the ruby red pulp. That was Sicily, always surprising you with its vibrancy. Of course, I was passionately in love at the time and everything seemed bright and intense— especially in contrast to England, where Gray and I had been living for several years by that time on account of the blacklist. I swear it had rained every single day we'd been in London. I'd grown accustomed to the dreariness, everything subdued, even the kitten I found near our flat in Soho, a pitiful blue Persian with copper eyes.

"Her name is Fog," I informed my brother, "and we're keeping her." Not that he would have denied me anything at that point in our bleak exile. I was seventeen when we arrived and had just given up my newborn son for adoption. I was desperate for something to love. As was he, poor Gray, although being seventeen, I thought only about my own sorrows.

Geoffrey was wearing a khaki jacket over baggy shorts, one of those belted safari outfits with multiple pockets. He looked like an insect, a grasshopper, maybe, his spindly legs folded awkwardly beneath him, Indian fashion. That's what they called it then, Indian fashion, and I imagined him as an American Indian, sitting cross-legged on the ground. But Geoffrey was being the other kind of Indian, the Hindu kind. Every morning he did an hour of yoga, followed by a dip in the pool, *au naturel*. He was before his time, a visionary. I'll give him that. Walden Lodge is now a fashionable spa where celebrities go to lose weight and detox. Clothing is optional, I've heard, and yoga is all the rage.

I drew the mink coat over my head like a hood and tied the sleeves around my neck, to free up my paws for pouncing. With a snarl, I launched myself at Geoffrey, catching him squarely in the middle of his chest and knocking him backward onto the ground.

"Ouf!" he gasped. "I've just been attacked by a . . . what kind of creature are you, Cara child?"

"I'm a cheetah. I'm extremely fast. You didn't have a chance," I consoled him as I brushed him off and helped him resume his yogi pose.

"A cheetah?" He still sounded a bit winded. "Are cheetahs native to this region? If so, it's the first I've heard of it." Geoffrey once told me that he'd been picked on at school for being a know-it-all.

"Very well. I'm a puma, then. I'm still pretty fast and I've been known to eat humans. In one sitting."

He extracted his monogrammed cigarette case from a pocket. "Do you mind? I always smoke at times like this," he said. "Calms the nerves."

Strange, now that I think of it. Those were his exact words when I found him standing over Vivien's body.

CHAPTER TWO:
CORONATION DAY
LONDON, ENGLAND, JUNE 2, 1953

The news that Edmund Hillary and his Sherpa guide had reached the summit of Mt. Everest reached us on the morning of Coronation Day.

"A crowning homage," said Geoffrey, reading aloud from the *Times*. "Those were Her Majesty's exact words."

"Delivered with her characteristic insouciance," my brother quipped.

Geoffrey sent him a withering look across the breakfast table. He'd flown out from L.A. especially for the occasion and would be seated among the peers in Westminster Abbey—he and some seven thousand others. Packed like sardines in their ermine capes and coronets for what promised to be an interminable ceremony. But Geoffrey was smitten with Elizabeth and would have endured far worse on her behalf.

"She's stunning, isn't she?" he said, admiring the portrait of the young queen on the cover of the *Illustrated London News*, the quiet elegance of her white gown offset by sparkling diamonds at her ears and throat. He passed the magazine across the table, to give me a closer look.

Gray and I were used to it by then, the way Geoffrey's aristocratic heritage reasserted itself the moment he set foot on British soil. The first time we'd seen the transformation was when he'd brought us to London two years earlier. This was not long after they'd convinced me to give up the baby, "they" being the studio people, who couldn't afford to have their screen idol involved in yet another scandal, and with a minor, no less. I did as I was told, stayed in seclusion at the lodge once my *condition* became obvious, gave birth in a private clinic without revealing the baby's father's name, held our son just long enough to register the tiny cleft in his tiny chin. Taylor's chin.

"Honey, you made a mistake, falling in love with me," he'd said, not unkindly, the day I told him that I was expecting. As if I had a choice! Honestly, what girl growing up on Hollywood movies in the 1940s didn't adore Taylor Reed? The devilish smile, that worldly air. The thrill he conveyed on the screen was nothing compared to Taylor's romantic intensity in the flesh. I thought I'd found true love, but mine was just another in the long trail of broken hearts he left behind. One of the less illustrious hearts. A passing fancy, if the truth be told, not even a proper affair.

Father blamed himself. The "seduction" had happened right under his nose, on the set of one of his pictures. "I haven't been a very good father, have I, Carissa? But I'll take care of everything, don't you worry."

I might have liked it better if he'd threatened to throw me out of the house. Then I could have run back to Taylor and begged him to make an honest woman of me. Mrs. Taylor Reed. Once he saw his son, I was certain he'd have turned over a new leaf.

Oh, but how could I have given my son away? The thought tormented me in the weeks after I gave birth. I hadn't realized I'd feel so attached to the baby when I'd agreed to the adoption. All I could think about was the shame of being an unwed mother, but in the brief instant I held my son in my arms, I knew I'd made a terrible mistake. For months I'd been carrying on a conversation with my unborn child inside my head. He'd become part of my life without my realizing it. Now I was all alone and Gray, my best friend and confidante since Vivien died, had problems of his own.

While I was embroiled in my sorry little melodrama, the kind they'd stopped making in Hollywood, thanks to the Hays Code, he'd been placed under surveillance by the FBI. During the entire period he insisted on calling my "confinement," my brother was holed up with me at the lodge, working on an adaptation of *The Brothers Karamazov*, which served only to deepen the government's suspicion that he harbored Communist sympathies since Dostoevsky, being Russian, was beloved of the Left. In fact, he'd been named to the House Committee on Un-American Activities, named several times, we later learned, on account of his youthful support of the Spanish Republic. At some point he realized our phone was tapped, but it hardly mattered since the studios had stopped calling. Even his television work dried up, and without work, my brother was truly miserable.

The day they issued the subpoena, Father bought three first-class tickets on the *Queen Mary:* one for Gray, one for me, and one for Geoffrey, who had volunteered to see us safely settled in England. "In times of crisis, geographical distance is just the thing," our chaperone blithely assured us. We had no time to think it over; we were sailing from New York in a week. I was too listless to put up resistance. All I could think of was the baby. Gray wasn't much better, alcohol being his painkiller of choice, then and always. Before we knew it, we were being bundled onto the train, shuttled across the country to be met at the station by a limousine and conveyed to The Pierre on Central Park, where father kept a suite. Two days later, we sailed for Southampton.

Geoffrey's new side emerged on the voyage. Virtually from the minute we boarded the *Queen Mary,* our chaperone exhibited an imperiousness with porters, pursers, waiters, stewards, sommeliers, and the like so natural that it must have been ingrained, along with a taste for luxury strikingly at odds with his abstemious California persona.

"Let's have the Dover sole, and a bottle of Chassagne Montrachet, shall we? No, not the 'forty-six. An unfortunate vintage," he confided to Gray, who had downed two martinis in the time it took Geoffrey to peruse the ship's wine list—this on top of the whiskey he'd consumed in his cabin—and was clearly in no condition to notice, let alone care.

The closer we drew to England, the more pronounced Geoffrey's aristocratic bearing became, and the more deference the ship's personnel showed toward our party. Initially, it had been the Walden name that mattered: Gray the son and me the daughter of the famous director, Robbie Walden; my status as the daughter of the actress Vivien Grant, who'd died so tragically, and so young, lending us added cachet. Geoffrey's literary reputation counted for little alongside the celebrity we represented, even if ours was largely reflected glory.

But within the staunchly British confines of the ship, Geoffrey was the star, not us. The Bryce-Jones pedigree did the trick; Geoffrey's grandfather had served as a cabinet minister during the reign of Queen Victoria and his elder brother, a renowned mathematician, sat in the House of Lords. Among the first-class passengers with whom we dined were the Duke and Duchess of Hampden, who had been present at Geoffrey's christening, and a Marquess with whom he'd gone up to Oxford, a jolly-old-chap of a fellow who insisted on being called "Pinky."

Pinky and Geoffrey stayed up all night reminiscing over brandy and cigars. Breakfast found them none the worse for wear, however; each morning they attacked their kidneys and kippers with gusto, whereas poor Gray could barely manage a cup of weak tea and a poached egg. I stuck to coffee and toast in an effort to lose the weight I'd gained during pregnancy. We marveled at the transformation in our friend. Gone was the air of distraction, the mystic's pose.

"Do you think everyone calls him Pinky, or just his school chums?" my brother wondered aloud. Mornings were generally his best time.

"Did you hear what Pinky calls him?"

Gray took a swallow of tepid tea and winced as if it were medicine. "How can the Brits drink this stuff?"

"He calls him 'Bum-Bum,' " I pursued.

"Cara!"

"It's true," I protested, feeling every bit the adolescent I pretended not to be.

"I am aware of the nickname, but you don't need to parade that smutty information at the breakfast table." Fifteen years my senior—his mother was Father's first wife, mine was his third—Gray sometimes took the job of older brother a bit too much to heart.

"What's smutty about it? I thought it was funny."

"Never mind. Finish your toast."

It was as if there were two Geoffreys on board the *Queen Mary*. The Geoffrey we knew kept up the practice of a morning swim, a bathing suit for propriety's sake his sole protection against the elements, and could still be found meditating in the privacy of his cabin wearing nothing more than a loincloth. The other Geoffrey dressed for dinner in a tuxedo, though its cut dated it to another era. When the orchestra struck up a waltz, he was one of the first on the dance floor and he danced quite well, with a grace uncommon in someone so tall. Women flocked to him and he seemed to enjoy the attention, whereas at Walden Lodge he'd been indifferent to female charm.

Over the course of the six-day crossing, the suave Geoffrey gradually supplanted the Geoffrey we knew. By the time we disembarked, Gray and I were the traveling companions not of a gangly intellectual with the abstracted air of a Hindu holy man, but of a self-assured scion of the British aristocracy, a Bryce-Jones able and willing to assume his place as a member of the ruling class.

Initially we made for the family estate in Surrey, where Geoffrey's brother William (the Earl) resided between terms. My expectations of English country houses had been formed, I will admit, by the sort of costume dramas that MGM and 20th Century Fox produced and our father directed—*Jane Eyre, Pride and Prejudice, Wuthering Heights*—these last two starring Laurence Olivier, my all-time favorite actor next to Taylor.

The Bryce-Jones property was stately enough to have served as a backdrop in any of them, but in close-up it left much to be desired. The furnishings were drab, curtains frayed, rugs worn in patterns traced by centuries of feet treading the same paths from door to window, bookshelf to one of the overstuffed chairs flanking the fireplace. Everything was coated in a layer of dust, entire wings were closed, the furnishings draped in sheets, and the windows hadn't been cleaned in ages, which made the interior spaces, already gloomy in the sparse light, dimmer still. The place resembled the set of an Edgar Allen Poe horror story, the kind featuring Vincent Price in his later years.

The war had changed everything and, although he tried to hide it, Geoffrey was plainly disconcerted by the shabbiness of his childhood home. Rationing was still in effect when we arrived, and labor shortages made it difficult to find decent servants, let alone afford them. William and his wife, whom even he addressed as Lady Emily, couldn't have been more gracious, but kicking around the cavernous estate was sad and we soon left for London, for digs in Soho, the empty flat of some Bryce-Jones relation who was wintering in Tangiers.

"What kind of person did you say he was, this second cousin of yours?" Gray wanted to know. The flat showed signs of having been the scene of raucous parties, although not recently.

15

Beneath the dust and grime, we discovered ashtrays overflowing with lipstick-tinged cigarette butts, half-empty beer mugs, plates and teacups stacked in the sink, champagne bottles under the couch. The bedrooms were littered with discarded evening wear, both men's and women's clothing, some of it quite pricey.

"Maybe they were in the middle of a party when the air raid siren went off, and they all went down into the shelter and were obliterated by a V-2," I suggested. The place appalled me and I had no intention of living amid such squalor.

Geoffrey—the new Geoffrey—feigned shock (shock was not in the old Geoffrey's repertoire, and neither was feigning). "Dreadful thought! Martin's parties tended to attract the cream of literary and artistic society. The progress of British culture in the second half of the twentieth century would suffer immeasurably." He paused and inserted a cigarette into the ivory holder he'd taken to using, picked up a lighter from one of the end tables and lit it, inhaled thoughtfully and returned to the matter at hand.

"Let me amend that. The course of British painting would be set back, without a doubt. British poetry, on the other hand, might profit from the absence of certain so-called men of letters." Geoffrey drew another ruminative puff. "He is not a second cousin, by the way. He is the only son of my uncle's second wife, who disinherited the children of his first wife and passed the entire fortune onto Martin. I'm not quite certain what that makes him."

The faintest trace of a smile came to Gray's lips. "A sitting duck?" he ventured.

"Hmmm, yes. Might explain the itinerant lifestyle," said Geoffrey, tipping ashes into an overfull ashtray. "I do think we need a charwoman rather urgently."

★ ★ ★ ★ ★

I'd never have admitted it in front of my brother, but I shared Geoffrey's fascination with the British monarchy. The very day he arrived from America for the coronation, we'd gone, all three of us, to the opening of *Young Bess,* a picture about the first Queen Elizabeth starring Jean Simmons as Bess and Stewart Granger as Thomas Seymour. Back at the flat, Gray began reciting some of the more ludicrous bits of dialogue from memory.

" 'Born at a time when heads were falling around her like cabbage stalks . . .' "

Before long, Geoffrey was feeding him lines. " 'You mean Bloody Mary is dying? She'll be dead by morning?' " This delivered in a spluttering imitation of Mr. Parry, the elderly caretaker at Hatfield, the country estate where Bess was banished after her mother's beheading.

" 'Dead as a doornail,' " Gray confirmed in the fluting falsetto of Bess's governess, the stalwart Mrs. Ashley.

I did my best to ignore them. In fact, I'd loved the film and had memorized a few bits of dialogue myself. "How was a girl of her age able to hold a man like that?" Bess asked her tutor, referring to Cleopatra and Caesar but thinking, obviously, of Tom Seymour. How indeed? But it wasn't simply the parallel to my own broken romance that enthralled me. Early on, when Tom was trying to persuade Bess to accompany him to Henry VIII's court, he let on that he'd admired her mother, Anne Boleyn.

"Her eyes," he said. "The same slim nose . . . but where's her smile? Do you know she turned men's heads with that smile?"

In real life, Simmons and Granger were married and you could feel the charge in their intimate scenes. I'm told that it was the same with *The Red Rose,* the silent film my father directed that launched my mother's career. Wasn't it Bette Davis who noted, in regard to her performance in *Jezebel,* how an affair between a star and her director produces electricity that the audience feels?

My mother was sixteen when she met Father. All his wives were young, but my mother, by all accounts, was special. The only woman he truly loved or, as Gray would have it, the only one he never cheated on; his own mother had put up with our father's philandering for years before he divorced her to marry wife number two.

I watched *The Red Rose* dozens of times in Father's screening room, trying to get a sense of the person my mother had been when she was my age. I was just ten when she died and for years afterward every mention of Vivien, no matter how trivial, brought me back to the sight of her drowned body floating in the pool in her nightgown, her long dark hair spread cloud-like about her head. The image was seared in my brain, crowding out all the tender memories of early childhood.

Geoffrey was frozen in place next to the swimming pool, a towel wrapped around his waist, his plans for a morning swim abandoned. He appeared distracted, but at the sound of my cries he turned, white-faced, put an arm around my shoulder and drew me close to his side.

"Do you mind?" he said, stooping to retrieve his pack of cigarettes from the ground. "I always smoke at times like this. Calms the nerves."

The ambulance crew was already heading toward us across the grass and we watched in silence as the men waded into the shallow end and fished my mother out, placing her onto a stretcher and covering her body with a sheet. I got a good look at her bloated face, and was oddly reassured by the sight. It wasn't her. Someone who resembled my mother, and wearing her nightgown, had somehow ended up in the pool, but any minute the real Vivien would appear.

Father came running out of the lodge, closely trailed by Jobo, his Japanese houseboy. "What's Cara doing here? Take her away, for God's sake!" he shouted.

The next thing I remember is sitting beside Geoffrey on the daybed in the cabana by the pool, both of us being ministered to by Jobo. He'd made us tea, but neither of us had drunk any; I suppose we were in shock. Father appeared in the doorway looking older than his fifty-one years. His expression said it all: Vivien was gone. I ran to him and he gathered me up in his arms.

"Your mother had an accident," he said, struggling to keep a hold on himself.

"An accident?" Geoffrey interrupted. "Good God!"

Father silenced him with a wave of his hand. "They're waiting for you at the lodge. They'll want a statement." Then it registered that Geoffrey was wearing nothing more than a towel. "Go with him," he told Jobo, "And make sure he puts some trousers on first."

When they'd left, Father broke down completely. "Carissa, my sweet girl. I'm so sorry. So very sorry," I heard him say between sobs, mine and his. ". . . my fault. All my fault."

They tried to hide it from me, the ugly rumors surrounding her death, but the death of Vivien Grant was in all the papers and I could read, after all. She was a Red, I learned, and had been seen in the company of dangerous men, Russian spies possibly. Hollywood at that time was rife with them. I didn't know what a Red was. Even after one of my classmates explained it to me, I had difficulty imagining my glamorous mother consorting with bearded revolutionaries—foreigners, the vodka-drinking sort, rough men who'd sooner slit your throat than risk exposing their treacherous plots, according to my fifth-grade source.

One tabloid suggested that Vivien had been involved in one of those plots, that she might have been murdered because she knew too much and was threatening to expose her associates to the FBI, but the only evidence for this contention was a witness who claimed to have seen her earlier that day in the company of a "mysterious man," the two of them huddled together over cocktails in some seedy lounge. *Last person to see Vivien Grant alive?* read the headline.

"Balderdash!" scoffed Geoffrey when I asked him about the story. "Those tabloids will stop at nothing to sell newspapers."

I suppose a part of me would have been satisfied if my mother had been murdered by one of her bearded co-conspirators, because then I'd have known for a fact that she hadn't wanted to die. I held it against her for a long time, you see, her leaving me so suddenly, and so completely. You might say it became my quest, to solve the mystery of her death—not for the sake of justice, but out of a deeper need to understand why I'd been abandoned. Of course I knew she didn't drown on purpose, but I blamed her all the same. What was she doing, wandering the grounds in the early morning hours in her nightgown, practically willing an accident to happen? If she loved me, couldn't she have kept herself out of harm's way? Beneath this loomed another, darker question: Was it my fault that she didn't love me enough to stay in my life?

Gray and I got to know a couple of bearded revolutionaries of the vodka-drinking sort during our exile in England, but they weren't rough once you got to know them. We'd settled into Martin's flat with Geoffrey; cleaned up it was surprisingly comfortable, and roomy enough for all three of us plus the kitten. Fog made it feel like home. Within a day or two of adopting us, she'd picked out her favorite places, and I soon grew accustomed to waking up with her curled into an apostrophe on the pillow beside me, or greeting her in the love seat when we came in from one of the edifying cultural excursions Geoffrey had planned.

At first Gray and I objected to being frog-marched through London's venerable museums, a captive audience for Geoffrey's impromptu lectures on Nabu, the god of scribes in ancient Babylon, who is depicted riding on the back of a snake-dragon, on ritual practices among the Assyrians and the seventh-century B.C. epic of *Gilgamesh*. The man's mind was like a trashcan heaped full of arcane knowledge, Mesopotamia apparently being the topmost layer—if only because this was the gallery in which we happened to pause during our first foray into the British Museum.

By the time we'd progressed from archeology to art, from pottery shards to stone tablets, relief carvings to burial objects, bronze figurines, and paintings, my brother and I had stopped behaving like recalcitrant schoolchildren. Gray, in fact, had become enamored with the art of the Mughal dynasty. One work in particular fascinated him: a miniature commissioned by the emperor Akbar from a children's fable, a dreamlike weaving of animals and mythological creatures, tigers, elephants, scorpions, vultures, dragons and an immense peacock-like thing with a dog's head known as a simurgh. On the spot, he composed a poem to it:

SIMURGH

"A bird with teeth
"copper feathers
"and lion's claws, her face
"wise, canine.

"She has seen the ages pass.

"Roosting in the tree of life which floats
"in the world sea
"she takes flight on the winds of Vavu-Vata.

"One day she will plunge into flames."

"Did you know they're afraid of snakes?" said Geoffrey.

"Really? I wonder if I can work that in somehow."

" 'The winds of Vavu-Vata,' " I recited, feeling the vibrations resonate pleasantly in the back of my throat. "Vavu-Vata. Vavu-Vata."

We were fine by then, the two of us. Gray and me. I'd discovered my own talisman in the National Gallery, of all places. A painting by Titian. I'd learned about Titian from Vasari's *Lives of the Most Famous Artists,* one of the texts I'd been assigned in the fancy East Coast boarding school Father sent me to. I knew that he was regarded as the greatest Venetian painter during the Renaissance, that his patrons included not only the Italian nobility, but emperors and popes. Nothing I'd read in Vasari had led me to suspect that a single work by the artist completed early in his career, and by no means regarded as a masterpiece, would stop me in my tracks and reduce me to tears, but this is what happened when I saw the *Noli me Tangere.*

Let no one touch me: Christ's words to Mary Magdalen, conveyed in Titian's rendering with infinite compassion. You see the Magdalen, one arm outstretched, arrested, her hand just inches away from the hand of her beloved. On her face Titian captured an expression of awe and agony combined; she thought she'd lost him but then he appeared, carrying the tools of a gardener, still clothed in his burial shroud, the wound visible on his right foot. In her astonishment, she has fallen to her knees as if pleading with him not to leave her again, but already he is turning away. He is remote, inaccessible, and yet in his downcast eyes I sensed regret. Regret for the pain he'd caused, along with a sorrowful awareness of all he meant to her. Acknowledgment, too, of the suffering she'd undergone on his behalf.

It consoled me, the painting. Everything I'd wanted from Taylor was contained in the expression on Christ's face. Gray saw my tears and seemed to know what I was feeling. "Ah,

Cara," he said, patting my shoulder sympathetically. Truly, he was the only person who understood me since Vivien died.

When he wasn't shepherding us through museums, Geoffrey was busy renewing his British connections. He bought himself an appointment book—a diary, as the British call it—a swank volume bound in Italian leather, and spent the mornings filling it with theater dates, luncheons, teas, and dinner parties. Literary people began dropping by the flat for sherry in the late afternoon, tweedy men with greasy hair and batty old ladies who reminded me of Miss Havisham in *Great Expectations.* Gray and I learned to make ourselves scarce during these occasions. The new Geoffrey tended to treat us like hired help, sending Gray out to the off-license to pick up more drink while I was pressed into service emptying ashtrays since most of Geoffrey's friends smoked as furiously as he did.

George Orwell died midway through January of our first London winter. He'd published a scathing attack on Geoffrey during the war, accusing him and other British pacifists then residing in the United States of abandoning their country in its hour of need and supporting the enemy. In a letter to the *Times* published alongside other tributes to the late writer, Geoffrey claimed that they'd made it up in recent years. Orwell regretted his words; the two had corresponded, in fact, and were entirely in agreement on the principle of pacifism, the right to nonviolent protest, particularly in the light of Gandhi's example. Their final exchange concerned *1984:* "I averred that its anti-totalitarian message was too strong," wrote Geoffrey. "I pray that I am proven right."

Geoffrey's letter provoked outrage in the letters column of the *Times,* spilling over into the less-reputable dailies. Orwell's admirers, particularly those who applauded the writer's anti-Communist stance, called him a coward. Some letter writers went so far as to accuse him of having been a Nazi sympathizer and there were even calls for his deportation. Attendance at sherry hours dwindled considerably, and blank pages began to appear in Geoffrey's diary with distressing frequency. But from the left-wing *Manchester Guardian* came an invitation to an evening forum marking the tenth anniversary of the English publication of Leon Trotsky's biography of Stalin.

Gray was keen to attend. "I'm accused of being a Communist. I think it's time I met some of my fellow travelers."

"Consorting with Trotskyists? Do you think that's wise?" Geoffrey fretted. "You're already *persona non grata* in the States."

"You don't have to attend. I'll make your excuses, if you like."

The event was held in a bookstore on one of the side streets leading away from the British Museum. We'd probably walked past it several times en route to one or another of our edifying cultural excursions, but it wasn't the kind of place you'd notice. There were no books in the window, no sign out front, nothing to lure customers in. Inside there were no shelves, just books stacked haphazardly on every available surface or piled on the floor.

I'd come to expect dimly lit, under-heated spaces in England, had taken to wearing two sweaters under my coat when we were invited out and rarely removed my coat indoors unless I could angle a spot for myself next to the fireplace or heater. Gray's fellow travelers—there were maybe a dozen of them in the room when we arrived—had all kept their coats on too I noticed, as if prepared to cut out at a moment's notice. A furtive air hung about the gathering. Geoffrey took one look at the scruffy little group and fled.

My brother made himself at home. Within moments of entering the bookstore he'd attached himself to a pair of bearded men with foreign accents, and the three of them began debating the show trials in Eastern Europe with relish. I couldn't follow their conversation and regretted not having gone home with Geoffrey.

"Are you with the New Left Book Club?" An unshaven fellow in a crumpled black turtleneck sweater was standing quite close to me, close enough for me to identify the components of his body odor. British people didn't wash very often and tended to wear the same clothes, day in, day out. (At that time, I was still blissfully unaware of the practice of sharing bathwater.)

"Um, no."

"I didn't think so. Those women tend to have mustaches."

"I've found that to be true of literary women in general in your country," I told him.

He laughed. "American?"

"Yes."

"James Hudson," he extended a hand. "What are you doing here, if you don't mind my asking?"

I shook his hand and tried to get past the body odor, to give him a second look. He was fairly handsome, in a Jimmy Cagney way. Intense, but with a nice smile. "Cara Walden. Do you mean what am I doing *here* here, or what am I doing in England?"

"Both, actually."

"I came to England with my brother," I said, gesturing toward Gray and the bearded foreigners. The room was beginning to fill and the three of them were now huddled in the far corner, still arguing. "He's a screenwriter. In Hollywood." I dropped my voice to a conspiratorial whisper. "We had to get out of America. He's been blacklisted . . ."

My companion's mouth fell open. "That dashing chap over there with the Russians? A writer, you say? I thought he was a film star." He took my arm and together we threaded our way through the crowd to Gray's little cluster. It was true. My brother was terribly handsome.

"Dmitri," James said, tapping the burlier of two bearded men on the shoulder. "Do you know who you're talking to?"

"I have not his name, no. But name is not important. He is my comrade." Dmitri thumped my brother on the back. "He knows my country, the great soul of the Russian people. He admires Dostoevsky."

Gray shrugged. The third man looked at his feet, evidently embarrassed by his friend's effusiveness.

"This man is a hero," James said. "The American government is after him. He's on the blacklist."

"You are persecuted American Communist!" Dmitri exclaimed, crushing my brother against his ample chest in a bear hug. "Comrade!"

"I'm sorry, Dmitri," said Gray, disentangling himself with some difficulty from the Russian's embrace. "My government thinks everybody in Hollywood's a Communist. All I did was support the Popular Front."

"Supported it when?" the third man asked suspiciously, glowering at Gray from beneath his bushy eyebrows.

"Not now, Ivo," said James, his voice taking on a bit of an edge. "Would you gentlemen mind if I took your comrade with me?" Without waiting for a response, he led us to the back of the store, where a few people were setting up a podium and arranging chairs in rows.

Gray was welcomed as a visiting dignitary. When at long last the program got underway, he was introduced as "our blacklisted American colleague" and received a polite round of applause. I hadn't believed the accusations about my brother's subversive politics. During the war he'd made patriotic films for the Air Force, for goodness sake—hardly the act of an enemy of the state—but it was obvious from his rapt attention to the proceedings that he was well informed on the events of the Russian Revolution and the nasty in-fighting that followed the glorious proclamation of the workers' state.

For my part, I must confess, the audience interested me far more than the lecture. So this is what Communists look like, I thought to myself, surveying the room. Dmitri and Ivo notwithstanding, beards were in short supply, but most of the men and women wore eyeglasses—the crowd was decidedly intellectual—and from the pallor of their skin, I surmised that they spent most of their time indoors. Not that I blamed them. What I would have given for a day of California sunshine!

Afterward a bunch of us went off to a nearby pub. It was coming on closing time, so instead of ordering just one pint, everyone ordered two. Or three. As the guest of honor, Gray was treated to many pints; the collection of beer glasses in front of him was truly alarming and I worried how I would get him home. Fortunately, he was too busy answering questions about the McCarthy hearings to drink them all.

James and I took a small table at some remove from the others. I gave him an edited version of my life, leaving out Taylor and the baby, focusing instead on the dubious benefits of belonging to a famous family. James's background, as it turned out, was not unlike Geoffrey's. His ancestors were also landed gentry, but in the north of England. One of them in the last century had owned a mine.

"Our family's fortune was built and maintained on the backs of the working class," he said, shame-faced. "I was sent to public school and university on that money."

Such self-recrimination was new to me. "You can't help what your great-great grandfather did. It's not as if you personally exploited people."

"Who I am personally doesn't matter. I'm part of an exploitative class system." He took a swallow of beer. "Surely you've read Karl Marx."

"I read Aristotle and Plato. Boccaccio too, in Italian. And

Shakespeare." Marx wasn't on the syllabus at the Wentworth Academy for Young Ladies.

"Plato was a proto-fascist and Aristotle consorted with imperialists. There's good stuff in Boccaccio and Shakespeare, if you know where to look. You really ought to read Marx, though. I can lend you a copy if you'd like."

"Are you allowed to buy Karl Marx's books in England?" I asked Geoffrey at breakfast the next morning as he was buttering his toast.

"Of course you are. I can assure you there is no House Committee on Un-American Activities on these shores," he responded through a mouthful of toast. "Listen to the child," he added in an aside to Gray. "One night in the company of Trotskyists—and a seedy lot at that—and she's dying to read *Das Kapital.*"

"I'd recommend starting with the *Communist Manifesto,*" my brother said without looking up from his morning paper. He'd gotten out of bed and gone straight to the news agents to pick up a copy of the *Manchester Guardian,* a daily habit he would observe scrupulously from that point on. "This wouldn't have to do with that good-looking young man you were talking to in the pub, would it?"

James had asked for my phone number when we'd parted. I wanted to be better prepared before I saw him again. But if I saw him again, I hoped that he'd have found time to bathe, shave, and change his sweater.

"We did talk about Marx," I admitted. "He offered to lend me one of his books and invited me up to his room on the way home to get it, but I thought I'd just buy my own copy."

Geoffrey snorted. Bits of toast flew out of his mouth and scattered across the tablecloth. "Odd kind of courtship, wouldn't

you say? Young men in my day invited girls up to see their etch-
ings."

Gray saw more of James in the following weeks than I did,
which was fine with me. He wasn't my type, but he seemed to
be Gray's. The comrades, as we began calling them, met fairly
regularly in the little bookstore off Gower Street and my brother
found the gatherings congenial. Through these associations,
small writing commissions in obscure left-wing magazines began
to come his way, low-paying work, to be sure, but he seemed to
enjoy it. Nobody who read *Masses Unite!* associated the Gray
Walden who reviewed literature for that publication with the
Hollywood director who possessed the same last name.

I didn't share my brother's enthusiasm for the comrades and
couldn't make it beyond the first few pages of the *Communist
Manifesto*. Spending the evening with Fog, tucked up under an
afghan with an Agatha Christie, was far preferable to attending
a political gathering, but what I really loved was the London
stage. Geoffrey's tastes ran to the classics: we saw the Oliviers in
Antigone and made the trip to Stratford-upon-Avon a couple of
times that summer to see *Julius Caesar* and *Measure for Measure*
with John Gielgud and Peggy Ashcroft. At Gray's insistence, we
also saw plays by Chekhov and Ibsen. For all the depredations
of postwar England, British theater was still top notch, but the
more plays we saw, the more aware I became of my inadequacy
as an actress. The bit parts I'd played in Father's Hollywood
productions had required very little skill; I would need to study
the craft if I wanted to be taken seriously.

Geoffrey was undergoing a sobering self-analysis of his own.
Doors were not opening for him in the publishing world. A
good many of his former acquaintances shunned him; evidently
the Orwell tribute had not produced the effect he desired. In
the autumn, he went off to the Netherlands to attend the Twelfth
Congress of the International Vegetarian Union. We saw the

new Geoffrey off at the station, but it was the old Geoffrey who returned. A short time later, he was booking his passage home to California on a steamer, taking the long way back via India.

With Geoffrey gone, Gray and I reverted to our old ways. The dining room table became once again my brother's office as it had been at the lodge; the charwoman knew better than to move so much as a pencil or rearrange a single pile of paper. Other blacklisted Hollywood people had begun showing up in London, actors, writers, and directors with whom Gray had worked in the past, and our flat became a gathering place for exiled Americans.

Someone had the idea of adapting Gray's screenplay of *The Brothers Karamazov* as a play for the upcoming Festival of Britain. Rehearsals began in December and *Brothers* opened in the basement of a social hall in Soho and played for two weeks in May to enthusiastic audiences, including a surprising number of Russian émigrés, friends and relatives of Dmitri's. London Films optioned the script—the film was never made, unfortunately—but assignments from British studios started coming Gray's way. Some of the movies he worked on were intended for distribution in the United States; if Gray's name appeared in the credits, the film wouldn't be shown. We solved the problem by inventing a pseudonym for my brother: Johnnie Dash. The name suited him, with his shock of dark hair and the dapper little goatee he'd grown since coming to England, and he became known as Johnnie Dash in the expat community. I don't think he minded discarding the name of Walden one bit.

I worked behind the scenes on the production of *Brothers*, painting scenery, creating makeshift dressing rooms by stringing clotheslines to hang sheets over like they did in *It Happened One Night*, and prompting the actors at rehearsals when they forgot their lines. Dick Leppard was directing and he was tireless! Toward the end, we were rehearsing day and night, seven days a week. We'd leave the hall and head for one of the nearby jazz clubs that was open late and drink and dance until they threw us out. I'd picked up smoking, and applied my eyeliner with a liberal hand. It pleased me to be treated as a woman, not a girl, by the cast and crew. When I turned eighteen, nobody could believe how young I was.

The Archer was our favorite nightclub and we all went there to celebrate on opening night. I drank more than I should. People kept refilling my glass when I got up to dance and I just kept emptying it. When someone handed me a microphone, I stood up and sang "Embraceable You" in my best Judy Garland imitation. We'd seen her at the Palladium a month earlier and I was infatuated with her singing, her powerful yet fragile persona. "Embrace me, my sweet embraceable you." Naturally, I was thinking of Taylor and I poured my heart and soul into the song.

"That wasn't half-bad," said a portly man, who turned out to be Mr. Reggie, the club's manager.

"Why don't you book her?" Dick suggested. "She's a class act."

"How much do you want?"

The two of them negotiated a price for a three-week gig as I hovered uselessly on the sidelines, ignored by both. I didn't realize until Gray and I got back to the flat that Mr. Reggie thought Dick was my agent.

"I hope he doesn't expect a cut," my brother commented.

Chapter Three:
Dory

I haven't been entirely candid in my account so far. Not that I've lied outright, but I've left things out. Our musician friend Dory, for example, who arrived at the flat just as Geoffrey was setting off for Westminster Abbey. Those of us who didn't have aristocratic forebears would be watching the coronation on television. We had our own set and Gray, in his expansive Johnnie Dash persona, had invited everyone we knew. Actors, directors, musicians, screenwriters, the comrades, all crammed into our sitting room, with enough drink to float the Royal Navy.

But there, I'm doing it again, narrating events in the jaunty tone of a 1930s screwball comedy, complete with clever dialogue and stock characters beloved in films of that era: eccentric British aristocrat, colorful foreigners, including a pair of Russians straight out of *Ninotchka,* a struggling writer (Gray) destined for redemption by the picture's end, with myself in the role of ingénue. A slightly soiled ingénue, I'll grant you, but still naïve, however much I pretended otherwise. Dangerously naïve, if the truth be told.

I suppose I asked for it, tarted up in my borrowed finery. I had my pick of evening gowns from the jumble left in the flat: a black taffeta cocktail dress with a cinched waist and full circle skirt embroidered with a beaded rose design, a strapless number by Christian Dior in blue-green organza with a chiffon sash. My favorite was a sequined sarong with a plunging neckline, slit up to the middle of my thigh. I'd gotten a seamstress to take it in and it fit like my own skin. I wore my dark hair long in those days and tucked a gardenia behind one ear.

"You look like Dorothy Lamour," Gray said the first time I wore it.

"Is that a compliment?"

"You know Dorothy Lamour. She starred in all those "Road" pictures with Bob Hope and Bing Crosby . . ."

"You haven't answered my question."

My brother seemed on the verge of speaking, but thought better of it and went back to his *Guardian*.

"Why don't you like my dress?" I pouted.

"It's too old for you."

"That's the point, isn't it?"

We all wanted to look older, "we" being aspiring actresses trying to break into show business. Making your debut as an in-génue was considered the kiss of death as far as your future prospects were concerned. Bad-girl roles gave you so much more to work with, so it paid to look the part. And it was fun, adopting a risqué pose at the Archer, where nearly everyone was pretending to be someone else. I cultivated a jaded persona, steered clear of upbeat material, bright lyrics, anything hopeful, specializing instead in bitter songs in a minor key, ballads of impossible love, of illicit but inexorable desires. At the end of my set, admirers vied with one another to buy me drinks, all desperate to cheer me up, but their attentions got them nowhere. Offstage, I conveyed a yearning, like Greta Garbo in *Grand Hotel*, to be left alone.

Mr. Reggie lapped it up. I'd catch him watching me as I was doing my set. Like prey. He took his time, chose his moment well: a Saturday afternoon in the dead time before opening. I was working on a new number with the band and stayed around after the others left to watch a calypso group auditioning for a spot at the end of the program. I'd heard a lot of jazz but this was something else. The syncopated rhythms and bell-like clamor of the steel drums, the lilting Caribbean accent of the singer took me far away from dreary London. It wasn't only the carefree melodies, although I found them irresistible. The music made me want to dance barefoot in the grass the way I used to as a child at Walden Lodge, back in the days before my mother died.

"I hate to see a pretty girl dancing all by herself," said Mr. Reggie. He'd come up behind me while I was swaying to the beat of one of the songs and a moment later I found myself wrapped in his arms, pinned so tightly against him that I could feel his member pressing against my lower back. With one hand he began groping under my skirt while the other hand pawed my breast.

"No," I said, struggling to release myself from his grip. I elbowed him in the vicinity of his groin and had the satisfaction of making him wince.

"You're a feisty one," Mr. Reggie grunted, changing his hold so his arm was around my neck. I felt myself being lifted off the ground, gasping as his arm tightened across my windpipe. "Need a man to keep you in line, you do," he said. "Show you who's boss."

I somehow managed to free an arm and began flailing at him, kicking his shins with my high-heeled shoes, my frenzied exertions weirdly in sync with the lively rhythm of the steel drums playing off against the guitars and saxophone. All of a sudden the music stopped. Then I felt Mr. Reggie's grip loosen and I slipped out of his grasp just an instant before he fell to the floor.

"You don't dance with a lady when de lady say no," I heard a Caribbean-accented voice say. That was Dory. To look at him, you'd never have taken him for a hero. I don't mean because he

34

was black; it was his bearing I'm referring to, his courtly manners. You never saw him without a jacket and tie, his trilby hat and black umbrella. A proper British gentleman from head to toe. He wrote a song about it, actually, his allegiance to England. "My Mother Country," one of his earliest hits. But there was iron in him, along with a quiet dignity you couldn't help but admire.

Mr. Reggie got to his feet. "Get out," he spat. "The lot of you." He made a sweeping motion with his arm, including me in the gesture. Dory's fellow musicians were already packing up their instruments. I straightened my clothing, retrieved my coat and handbag from backstage, and followed them out to the street.

Was I trembling? Dory said I was, so it's probably true. I do remember that it was raining, but when wasn't it raining in England? "Come," he said, sheltering me under his umbrella. "We walk you home."

Gray and Dory hit it off immediately. They shared a bond, those two, an awareness of the unspoken rules that kept outsiders in their place. Dory stood out on account of his dark skin, but in another sense he was not seen in England. Not pictured in the advertisements, not featured in radio programs or films. Not parodied, as was true of black characters in American entertainment of that era, but as a man he seemed, somehow, not *there*. Would Mr. Reggie have made his move on me in full view of a group of white musicians?

Gray had the same problem, but in reverse. He blended in so long as he pretended to be like everyone else; he could "pass" as heterosexual. A thirty-five-year-old bachelor raised eyebrows in some quarters, to be sure, especially given how handsome my brother was, but he was discreet about his liaisons. And he had good reason to be: "perverts" like Burgess and Maclean cast suspicion on all left-leaning homosexuals. Their cowardice in

fleeing to the Soviet Union when they were about to be exposed
as spies was seen as part and parcel of their sexual immorality.
Stereotypes of fairies as lisping poets and swishy fashion design-
ers were everywhere in those days, but serious homosexuals—
men who openly loved other men, not flamboyantly, but
honestly and without shame—were publicly vilified and subject
to legal prosecution.

I see all of this only in retrospect. At the time, I was oblivious
to so much that went on around me. Well, not oblivious. I
noticed things, observant girl that I was, but failed to connect
the dots. Like Geoffrey, I lived in a world of my own, one that
coincided only occasionally with the world outside. But that
day, Coronation Day, the outside world came crashing in and
just like the day when my mother died, neither Geoffrey nor I
could ignore it.

The morning dawned dark and drizzly. Hardly a day to be out
and about in fancy dress, as Gray pointed out to Geoffrey.
"You'll look like a mangy animal, once that ermine gets wet."

"No matter," Geoffrey said serenely. "My escort always carries an umbrella."

Dory, who was at that very moment shaking the raindrops
from his umbrella in the foyer, gave him a delighted smile. "It
would be my pleasure."

"You can't be serious," my brother said.

Geoffrey adjusted his cape in the mirror. "There's ample
room in the Abbey. Lady Emily phoned this morning. William's
gout is acting up. They won't be coming down from Oxford.
Much too uncomfortable, all that standing up and sitting down."

"Don't be obtuse. It's not a question of making room in the
pew."

"Surely we can muster up some appropriate formal wear. The

flat is full of it. A tuxedo, perhaps?" He eyed Dory's muscular frame.

"Everyone will assume he's your manservant," Gray persisted. "Your exotic Caribbean manservant."

Once again, Dory's chivalry saved the day. "I am not wanting to be in de church, Geoffrey. I walk you dere and wait outside, to see Her Royal Highness."

"Nonsense!" Geoffrey protested, giving his appearance a final onceover. "A West Indian has as much right as a British-born subject to a place at the coronation. She's your queen too."

Gray laid a restraining hand on his shoulder. "This isn't the occasion for asserting your egalitarian principles."

"I wait outside," Dory repeated, his tone polite yet implacable. An unspoken exchange passed between him and Gray—a pained look on my brother's face, a shrug from Dory.

By the time Dory returned from the Mall, the party was in full swing. The coronation was still being broadcast but nobody was watching television. Dmitri had brought a balalaika and was running through his repertoire of Russian folk songs, accompanied by Ivo, who had a surprisingly rich baritone.

"Wonderful voice," I overheard one of the blacklisted American directors say.

"He used to be in the Red Army Choir," his wife informed him. "Sang for the troops at Stalingrad. He told me so."

Gray was weaving through the crowd, a bottle of gin in one hand, a bottle of whiskey in the other. "Who needs topping up?"

The director held out his glass. "Is it true?" he asked, pointing his chin at the Russian. "Was he a member of the Red Army Choir?"

"First I've heard of it," Gray said, splashing gin into the director's glass. "But with Ivo, who can say for sure? He's such a cypher." Just then he caught sight of Dory and beckoned him over. "So, how was it? Did you see Her Royal Highness?"

"Queen Elizabeth was splendid in her golden coach," Dory affirmed in all seriousness. "De Duke of Edinburgh was also very fine. Look, I show you." He pulled a folded handkerchief out of his trouser pocket and shook it open with a flourish. The handkerchief was decorated with a picture of Westminster Abbey in the center surrounded by crowns. A repeating pattern of golden carriages, each drawn by a team of horses and flanked by costumed footmen, proceeded merrily around the border.

"Her Majesty Queen Elizabeth the Second of the United Kingdom of Great Britain and Northern Ireland, Head of the Commonwealth," my brother read aloud. "Imagine fitting all that on a handkerchief!"

"Take it, please," Dory said, foisting the handkerchief upon him. "I have another."

"Thanks. I'll treasure it forever." It was a challenge for Gray to get the handkerchief into his own pocket with a bottle in each hand; he was fairly sloshed. I took the whiskey away from him before he spilled it on the carpet.

Our friend hadn't finished bestowing souvenirs. "This is for you, Cara." He gave me a silver teaspoon engraved with the date and the words *Vivat Regina,* its handle worked in the shape of a crown.

"Long live the queen," Gray murmured. Dory smiled.

"Vivat Regina," he repeated thoughtfully. "Vivat Regina." He hummed a jaunty five-syllable phrase, followed by another four syllables long. "Vivat Regina. Long live de queen. De loveliest lady I've ever seen. She is our ruler. Long may she reign. All hail Eliz'beth, our sovereign."

My brother clapped him on the back. "That's very good. Makes monarchism sound fun."

"Did you compose it on the spot?" the director's wife wanted to know.

Dory nodded. "De songs come to me like gifts. I start with a phrase and soon I have a symphony."

"How marvelous! Darling, you know the most fabulous people," she said to Gray. She took Dory's arm and attempted to lead him off. "Let's get Dmitri to pick it out on the balalaika. We can all sing along."

"Just one moment, if you don't mind," Dory said. He scanned the room, looking for Margaret. "Is she here, my princess?"

"She dropped in earlier," I told him, "on her way to work. The pub's open all day, you know. Special hours. She said she'd see you later."

Two years into our exile, I'd come to appreciate a few things about London, and The Crown and Two Chairmen, where Dory's girlfriend Margaret tended bar, was one of them. Decorated with Persian rugs and a hodge-podge of shabby armchairs, it felt like the lounge of an old-fashioned hotel, the sort of place you'd hole up in during a rainstorm, not intending to stay, but it grew on you. Karl Marx had lived next door and it wasn't hard to imagine him drinking in the upstairs bar, where streetwalkers and bohemian types of both sexes rubbed shoulders with former RAF pilots. Gray and the comrades liked to speculate about which armchair was his.

Dory's band played there two nights a week—he had three or four regular gigs in London by then—and over the course of several months, I'd watched him win her. Princess Margaret: she always laughed when he called her that, but I could tell she liked it. Sometimes Dory would catch her eye during a set, and you had the feeling that whatever he was singing from that point on was meant for her and her alone. The rest of us weren't supposed to be listening. "She is de girl, dis one you see. De girl who carries the heart of me."

I longed to find someone who'd love me like that.

★ ★ ★ ★ ★

By the time Geoffrey returned, the skies had cleared and Gray's party had spilled out of the flat and into the street, where it blended with the neighbors' parties. One big celebration, Union Jacks flying from the lampposts, bunting draped from one end of the street to the other, kids setting off firecrackers like on Guy Fawkes Day. From the moment he arrived, Geoffrey was right in the thick of things.

"It's that asinine cape," Gray said. "You'd think he was royalty, the way he's being feted." It looked to me as if the people on the street were honored to have a peer among them. I recognized a good performance when I saw one and besides, the role suited him. "He's just giving them what they want."

"Yes, I suppose so. He does the *noblesse oblige* routine very well," my brother admitted grudgingly.

This wasn't the first time I'd sensed tension between the two of them since Geoffrey's return to England—or not between the two of them, exactly. The animosity was all coming from Gray and as the evening progressed, I overheard snatches of conversation among the American expatriates, snide references to Geoffrey's testimony before the McCarthy Committee. He was, I learned, a friendly witness. He named names. "How else do you think he got back into the U.S.?" one of the blacklisted screenwriters said. "He was in the thick of it. A card-carrying member right from the start. It's a wonder they didn't deport him during the war."

I didn't know what to make of the allegation. Could Geoffrey have betrayed someone we knew? I could see it happening by accident, Geoffrey being indiscreet in mixed company, unaware that an FBI informer was listening, but deliberately to have given information to HUAC? Information that might have landed one of Gray's Hollywood friends in jail? The Geoffrey I'd known since childhood would never have stooped so low. I couldn't see him as a Communist, either, given his high-brow tastes.

At some point, as the festivities on the street were winding down, a group of us made our way to The Crown and Two Chairmen. Dory's band was already playing in the public bar and "Vivat Regina" was fast becoming a hit, judging from the number of times the patrons requested the song. Margaret was busy drawing pints for the thirsty celebrants—the place was packed—but she left her post long enough to bring over a tray of beers.

"First round's on the house tonight, love," she said, waving away the five-pound note Gray handed her.

"Keep it for the second round, then," my brother said. Margaret and I exchanged a look over his head. He'd been very sick that winter, from the smog. Thousands died from it; the skies were yellow and people were told to stay indoors, the air was so poisonous. And then, already weakened, he'd come down with the flu, which had turned into pneumonia. Margaret helped me nurse him through the worst, when every ragged breath he took sounded like his last. He owed us his life, he said, when he'd recovered sufficiently to joke about such things.

"So do us a favor," Margaret said. "Lay off the bloody drinking before you kill yourself right proper."

He took it from her when he'd never take it from me, but that night he was in no mood to take it from anybody. Geoffrey and I eventually succeeded in getting him home. The flat was a shambles, but the charwoman would be in the next morning. I said goodnight to Gray and Geoffrey, coaxed Fog out from under my bed, where she'd been hiding ever since the first guests arrived, fed her and brought her with me into the bathroom for company as I drew a bath.

I did my best thinking in the bathtub. A good long soak cleared my mind of clutter and allowed me to prepare for acting class. I'd auditioned for a studio in Notting Hill Gate run by the sister of a renowned classical actress. I wasn't sure I was up to the repertoire, being American and not particularly well versed in the theater, but the Wentworth Academy had instilled a solid enough grounding in Shakespeare to get me through.

Once in, however, I'd found that I needed to unlearn nearly everything I'd picked up from the movies. So much of Hollywood acting was about putting on a character, adding quirks and mannerisms on the outside as opposed to finding the essence within. I used to love the way Bette Davis smoked a cigarette, for instance, had the moves down even before I started smoking myself. Such style, the way she inhaled and moved the cigarette slowly away from her mouth before allowing the smoke to seep from her dark lips! Distracting. Everything about Bette Davis was over-staged, in the judgment of my teachers. One learns to subtract, I was told.

I may have drowsed for a bit in the bath. The sound of loud voices in the sitting room aroused me. By the time I'd toweled off, put on my robe and gathered Fog up in my arms, Vincent, Fitz, and Lord Trafalgar, the other members of Dory's band, were already in the middle of some story, all three talking at once. To my sluggish mind, the series of events they were relating made no sense.

Fitz: "He go to help her."

Vincent: "She say no, but he helping her anyway."

Lord Trafalgar: "Dey be calling her names."

Vincent: "Nigger's whore."

Gray interrupted. "Who was doing this? People in the pub?" He was stone sober, I noticed, and pacing the room like a caged animal.

"Dey boys. Young like her," Fitz said, inclining his head toward me. I saw that he was bleeding from a cut on his cheek. Vincent's face was bruised as well, and his jacket was torn and blood stained. Lord Trafalgar was in the worst shape, with a black eye and a bloody nose whose flow he was trying to staunch with a sodden handkerchief.

"Hooligans!" Geoffrey exclaimed.

I set Fog down on the carpet and went into the kitchen to get a clean dishtowel for Lord Trafalgar, who accepted it with a distracted nod. I went into the bathroom and got cotton, iodine, and a sticking plaster for Fitz.

"But I don't understand," Geoffrey was saying. I poured some iodine on a piece of cotton and applied it to Fitz's cheek. "Why were they picking on Margaret? What did she do? Refuse to serve them drinks?"

Fitz: "She kiss him. Ouch!"

"Oh, sorry," I said, trying to dab more gently at his cut.

Lord Trafalgar: "Inside, when we finish de set. Dey no like that, de kissing, she white and he black. But he make dem go outside."

Fitz: "He carry dem outside."

Vincent: "Throw dem, you mean."

I was beginning to get the picture. Margaret had kissed Dory in the pub and a couple of patrons took offense. Boys, Fitz had said. Punks, I amended in my head. The type who liked picking fights with immigrants. Cocky, preening, strutting in their long jackets and brocaded vests that made them look like gentlemen from another era, although they were anything but gentlemen. They'd soon have a name: Teddy Boys.

"Who made them go outside? Dory?" said Gray.

Lord Trafalgar: "Big Russian. Your friend."

Vincent resumed the story. "Dey be waiting outside, de boys. When we leave de place dey attack him and knock him down. Dey be kicking him but we pull dem off."

"Didn't anyone call the police?" Geoffrey wanted to know.

"Two bobbies watching de whole time," Lord Trafalgar affirmed matter-of-factly.

It dawned on me that our friend was the "him" who had taken the brunt of the beating. "Where's Dory?" I interrupted, alarmed.

"They took him to Middlesex Hospital," Gray said wearily. "Margaret went along." He'd stopped pacing and was standing next to the mantelpiece, one elbow propped on the ledge, resting his forehead in his palm. This was apparently the preamble I'd missed. I sank into the love seat, stunned.

"Will he be all right?" I looked into the eyes of Fitz, Lord Trafalgar, and Vincent, each in turn, and watched each of them glance away. "Please tell me. I want to know."

Vincent came to perch on the arm of the love seat. "Dis be his blood," he said sadly, pulling his jacket away from his body. I could see how it had soaked through to his shirt. "One of dem have a knife. I holding him until de ambulance come."

"Oh!" I said on a sharp inhalation, eyes filling with tears. Vincent leaned down and patted my back. I buried my face in my hands and wept, seeing Dory bleeding, cradled in his friend's arms. Dory lifted onto a stretcher and carried to a waiting ambulance. It all felt horribly familiar; then, as now, all I could do was wait for the bad news to come. Through my tears, I heard Geoffrey quizzing Lord Trafalgar about the bobbies.

"You don't mean to tell me the police saw what was happening and did nothing?"

"Yes, dat is what I say."

Geoffrey let out a huff of disbelief. "One hears of these things happening in the southern United States, but not in England."

"Why not in England?" my brother snapped. I looked up, startled by the sharpness of his tone. "This country's riddled with prejudice, on top of class bigotry. You'd know it if you didn't have your head up your ass most of the time."

"Well, I didn't mean . . ." Geoffrey fumbled with a pack of

cigarettes. "Of course we've had our share of difficulties, historically. The empire was always problematic, if you want my opinion," he said, removing a cigarette and inserting it between his lips. He felt in his pocket for a lighter.

"Damn problematic," Gray muttered.

Geoffrey continued as if he hadn't heard him. "But clearly the move toward independence for the colonies is a good thing, regardless of what the Tories say." He paused to light the cigarette, inhaled, and blew a cloud of smoke toward the ceiling. "I have every confidence that our subjects"—he gave a nod to Lord Trafalgar, Fitz, and Vincent—"will soon be governing themselves quite ably."

"*Our* subjects," Gray mimicked nastily. "Yours and the queen's? What patronizing crap!" He pounded the mantle with his fist. Beside me, I felt Vincent tense up. Fitz and Lord Trafalgar exchanged an anxious look. Nobody spoke.

I'd seen my brother angry on a number of occasions, but never enraged. Never teetering on the edge of violence, as he was now, blind with fury. During my "confinement," when we were both staying at the lodge, he'd buttonholed a studio head at one of Father's parties, challenged him for not standing up to the blacklist. "Are you going to let a bunch of paranoid right-wingers tell you how to run your business?" he had asked the man. "You're cutting your own throat, playing along with the McCarthy crew. Can't you see that?" He'd been drinking, of course, but even drunk, his belligerence was limited to verbal assaults; when incensed, he could be quite cutting, but I'd never seen him this passionate about anything. For the first time in my life, I was frightened in his presence, not knowing what he'd do next.

Geoffrey struggled to maintain his equanimity. "I'm not an apologist for colonialism," he said, drawing nervously on his cigarette. "Far from it. As for missionaries, I'd say they've got a lot to answer for, carrying Christianity into places where it was not wanted." He took another puff, warming to his subject. "Why, look at India. What do the Hindus want with the *King James Bible* when they've got the *Bhagavad Gita*? And the Chinese! One could study the Tao Te Ching for a lifetime and still not arrive at the bottom of it. Believe me, I speak from experience."

"Fuck your experience!" Gray strode across the room and for a moment I thought he was going to strike Geoffrey. So did Fitz, who moved as if to restrain him, laying a hand on his sleeve, but Gray shook it off and continued through to the foyer and out the door, slamming it shut behind him.

Next to me, Vincent exhaled. Geoffrey tamped out his cigarette in a saucer. It did feel as if we'd all been holding our breath, expecting something terrible to happen, but something terrible had already happened. Gray's outburst had distracted us from the real crisis, and his departure only temporarily relieved the tension in the room. Without him, however, the gathering became awkward. The Trinidadians seemed eager to get home; it was well after midnight and they all had day jobs.

Geoffrey insisted on walking them up to Oxford Street and putting them in a cab. While he was gone, I set to work restoring order to the flat. I was too upset about Dory to sleep, and on top of that I was worried about Gray. Where had he gone at this late hour in such a rage? The hospital was a possible destination, and it reassured me to think he might be headed there to wait with Margaret and bring back news of Dory's condition. I tried to convince myself that this was, in fact, the case as I collected bottles and glasses from the sitting room, emptied ashtrays, and moved the furniture, which we'd rearranged to face the television, back to its usual position. The alternative, that he'd ended up drinking somewhere, minus his regular companions, one or another of whom could at least be counted on to usher him home before he lost consciousness, was too worrisome to contemplate. I filled the kitchen sink with soapy water and started washing the glasses.

Neither Geoffrey nor I expected to sleep, but fatigue eventually overwhelmed us and we retired to our respective bedrooms. I was awakened by the sound of Mrs. Perkins vacuuming the sitting room with what struck me as unnecessary gusto.

"Had a party, did you?" she shouted over the noise as I wandered through on my way to the kitchen. The door to Gray's bedroom was ajar and I saw no sign that he'd returned. The bed, neatly made as always, still held a few of the guests' raincoats. No doubt they'd drop by during the course of the day to claim them.

Geoffrey appeared in the doorway, freshly shaved and dressed but careworn, his eyes red-rimmed and bloodshot, his face lined with fatigue. He looked elderly, which is not how I usually saw him. Growing up with his constant presence at the lodge, I'd never stopped to consider how old he was; he seemed to age very little from year to year, and he'd always been more of a playmate to me than an authority figure. But he'd served as an officer in World War I—the experience that had made him a pacifist—so he must have been somewhere around sixty. Younger than Father, but not by much.

I poured us each a cup of coffee. Geoffrey drank his standing up, one eye on the door to the flat, as if willing Gray to walk through it at any moment.

"We could go by the hospital," I suggested.

Geoffrey shook his head. He seemed to be in pain. "Your friend . . ." He stopped to clear his throat. "Our friend," he amended. "Dory . . ." He stopped again, sighed deeply, and came to sit down next to me at the breakfast table. "Cara, child. He passed away."

Chapter Four:
Out of Place

"No!" I think I might have shouted the word. Everything was too much all of a sudden. The morning light coming in through the kitchen windows: too bright. The smell of coffee grounds wafting up from the pot in front of me: too strong. The sound of Mrs. Perkins's vacuuming in the next room: too loud. I closed my eyes and covered my ears with my hands, blocking out the world. It wasn't true, I told myself inside my dark cocoon. How could Geoffrey be so sure? He barely knew Dory. It was a mistake. It had to be a mistake.

Geoffrey was attempting to pry my hands off my ears. "Cara," he said gently. I felt his fingertips on my cheeks, brushing away the tears. My face was wet with them, although I wasn't aware of crying.

"When?" I said eventually, wiping my eyes on the sleeve of my bathrobe.

"A few hours ago. Your brother called from the hospital." Geoffrey put two cigarettes in his mouth, lit them, and handed one to me. We smoked in silence for several minutes, during which time Mrs. Perkins ceased vacuuming and I was at last able to hear myself think.

On top of my own grief, I was worried about Gray. On some level I must have known that he would be shattered by Dory's death, although I wouldn't fully appreciate the depth of his feelings until somewhat later. No, it took Geoffrey to point it out. On occasion he could be remarkably perceptive, which made you wonder about all the other times when he did seem to miss the obvious.

The funeral service took place in a small church in Brixton. We three, plus Margaret, were the only whites in the place, but Fitz looked after us and afterward, in the basement social hall, he and Vincent and Lord Trafalgar sat with us as we drank cup after cup of milky tea served to us by the church ladies.

The shabby room was furnished with wooden tables and banged-up metal chairs that might've been in use since the industrial revolution; they had the look of factory equipment and were dreadfully uncomfortable. The windows still had blackout curtains, which gave the room an oppressive feel, as if we were waiting out a siege. Ordinarily I wouldn't have spent more than a minute in such dingy surroundings, but being with the band was the only way to keep hold of the fragile connection to our friend, and I don't think any of us were ready to let that go.

"What will you do now?" Geoffrey asked. Dory had been the heart of the band, the lead singer as well as the composer of most of their songs. It was hard to imagine them continuing without him, but Vincent said they would try.

"We play his songs. Dey be asking us to record some of dem."

Geoffrey was impressed. "Oh, well done! That might turn out to be rather lucrative."

"I don't know how we do it without him," said Fitz. I saw Lord Trafalgar nodding his head in agreement.

Vincent folded his arms across his chest and fixed the two of them with a stare. "We do it. For him, we do it."

"We no sing like him. Nobody pay to hear us," protested Lord Trafalgar.

Margaret gave me a nudge. "Cara sings, don't you, love?" The fellows looked at me expectantly.

"Oh, no. I couldn't. Really." I hated to disappoint them, but I wasn't up to the calypso repertoire. It wasn't my style, as I tried to explain while also fending off the attentions of one of the church ladies, who was attempting to refill my teacup yet again.

"You sing it your way," said Fitz. "We slow it down, like de Andrews Sisters."

"Rum and Coca-Cola," Vincent agreed. He hummed the chorus, and then launched into the first verse of the song, joined by the others. Up until this point Gray had been silent, lost in his own somber thoughts. I'd tried to draw him out a few times, but he remained distant, as he had been ever since his return from the hospital. What was going on beneath the surface was still a mystery to me, but the song lifted him out of his dark mood and it was seeing his sudden smile that made me go along with the idea.

We practiced together at the flat late at night, after I came home from class and when the fellows had gotten off work. Within a week or so we'd worked up half a dozen numbers, "Rum and Coca-Cola" chief among them, and Margaret arranged for us to try them out on a Wednesday night at The Crown and Two Chairmen. The audience for our debut performance consisted of Gray's blacklisted buddies, Ivo and Dmitri, and a handful of Trinidadians. I was introduced to Vincent's wife, whom I vaguely remembered meeting at Dory's funeral, and to Lord Trafalgar's sister Maxine.

I was wearing the sarong and had done up my hair in a French twist, with pin curls spilling across my forehead, Joan Crawford–style. I was trying to look cool and sophisticated, but inside I was a nervous wreck. Why had I let myself be talked into singing calypso? You needed an effervescent personality to pull it off, and a light touch with the material. Dory had that; I didn't. The minute the band started playing I was lost, memories of our friend standing where I was, his radiant presence, the sheer joy he took in singing his own lyrics, embroidering them as he went along—all of it engulfed me in sorrow, and fed a keen awareness of my inadequacy. I missed him too much to go on.

"Cara," hissed Vincent. "It's your cue." He was on steel pan, with Fitz on guitar. Lord Trafalgar was playing horn for this number, "Me Go Home Trinidad," a song Dory had written the previous winter, to cheer up Gray when he was sick.

Reluctantly, I opened my mouth and began to sing. "Me no sleep when de wind blow cold. No go out in de rain and snow. Icy winter make me feel bad. Me go home Trinidad." By the end of the stanza, I'd gotten the rhythm down and when Fitz and Vincent came in on the chorus, gratitude flooded my heart.

Dory's spirit was with us as we sang his song. We'd summoned him with his words and melody. I looked to the bar, where Margaret stood, one hand raised to pull a wineglass from the overhead rack. She'd paused, mid-motion, and I could see her lips moving. Emboldened, I invited the audience to sing along. "Go home. Go home. Me go back to de warm sunshine. Go home. Go home. Me go home Trinidad."

The night was a gift, we all agreed afterward. A healing balm for our wounded hearts. At the end of the performance, Vincent offered a prayer of thanks and I was pleased when my brother joined in, his voice firm as he repeated the final amen.

Father hadn't raised either of us in any particular religion. He'd left his own Jewish faith behind when he came to America after the First World War, a refugee from some remote province of Hungary. Walden wasn't the name he was born with, it was his Hollywood name, the one he chose when he first started working as a cameraman. His real name was something unpronounceable with an accent and too many consonants. Self-educated and thoroughly self-sufficient, he revered Thoreau as a saint. He'd built the lodge with his first million as a refuge from civilization and, of course, there was the nudity business, his own way of communing with nature, which Gray considered silly. But something of Father's vague spirituality must have gotten through, some reverence for the unknown, because my brother changed in the wake of Dory's death, taking on what I can only call, in retrospect, a kind of animism. Nature worship, but with a sinister cast: a summoning of primitive forces best left undisturbed.

The change in Gray occurred on Midsummer's Eve, the Saturday night immediately following our triumphant debut at the pub. There were open-air celebrations all over London, bonfires in the parks, with music and dancing. My fellow theater students and I staged a midnight performance of *A Midsummer Night's Dream* in Kensington Gardens, and it was four a.m. by the time I got back to the flat.

My first thought, upon seeing the hearty fellow drinking with Geoffrey in the sitting room, was that Puck himself had come to call. We'd had a rather fey Puck in our drama school production, a boy named Theo who hardly did the part justice. I'd imagined Puck as being more robust, a bon vivant type. No doubt Geoffrey had encouraged this reading of the character when he told me to envision him not as an endearing elf or fairy, but as a practical joker. "One of those people who starts out as the life of the party but soon grows tiresome. Very tiresome."

When Geoffrey introduced his cousin Martin, newly returned from his peregrinations in the Near East, I knew instantly that this was the very person he'd had in mind. Tousled hair—what there was of it—bow tie askew, belly protruding over the waist of his trousers, face flushed from the alcohol he'd imbibed, he did resemble a wayward deity, one who'd been demoted by his superiors for bad behavior. And he seemed to be taking Geoffrey down with him.

Martin rose unsteadily from his armchair. "Cara, is it? Charmed to meet you, my dear."

"Likewise," I said, shaking his proffered hand.

"Would you like a rum punch?" Geoffrey hiccupped. I looked at him in disbelief. I'd never seen him tipsy in all my nineteen years.

"No, thank you. I'm going to bed."

The two of them remonstrated with me loudly. Surely I didn't intend to sleep the day away, not on this of all days, the summer solstice. A glass of punch was just the thing to perk me up. We could all go to Stonehenge and do the thing properly, greet the dawn amongst the standing stones, like good pagans. They'd been waiting for me to get home before they roused Gray. We still had time to drive to Wiltshire if we left now; Martin had a car. I ignored them and made for the bathroom to remove my stage makeup. I'd played the role of Titania and we'd had to layer it on pretty thick to make me look matronly.

"Have it your way," Geoffrey called out petulantly. By the time I'd cleansed my face with cold cream and gotten into my pajamas, they were lurching out the door, en route to Stonehenge without me.

Fog emerged from my bedroom and mewed to be fed. I peeked into Gray's room as I passed by on my way to the kitchen and was relieved to see him sleeping soundly. That morning he'd learned of the Rosenbergs' execution, which had taken place the night before, well after midnight our time. Coming on top of Dory's death, the news hit him hard.

"I never thought they'd actually kill them," he said, shaking his head over the headlines of his *Guardian*.

Geoffrey'd looked up from the financial pages of the *Times*. "They were accused of treason, my dear boy. A capital offense."

"Their guilt wasn't proven."

"Ah, that's where you're mistaken. They were pink, weren't

they? Carrying on about injustice and whatnot? That makes them guilty in my book."

I could see my brother's color rising. "What was their crime? Wanting a better world? I thought you were on our side!"

"Which side would that be?"

"The side of the people, of course."

"Ah, that would be the losing side," said Geoffrey. Gray threw down his newspaper and got up from the table, but Geoffrey continued, unperturbed. "They were out of place," he sniffed in his reedy voice. "Next thing you know, they'd have been putting an end to segregation. Declaring a war on poverty. Giving inverts the right to marry and raise children. Good heavens! What a vision!"

During the course of the day, a number of Gray's Hollywood friends dropped by to commiserate. A few were Communist Party members who'd been picketing the American embassy in the days leading up to the execution. They were all for staging a mass demonstration. Communists in Paris and Rome were taking to the streets. Why shouldn't London's Communists join them? But other expatriates urged caution. The British were caught up in their own spy hysteria. If any of them were arrested, they were likely to be deported. Which was worse: lying low in England or (very likely) going to jail in America?

My brother sat passively through the debate, siding with neither faction. He seemed not to care one way or another; had the demonstrators won, I imagined he would have followed them out onto the streets, but the conservatives held sway and eventually the gathering broke up, the Communists grumbling about putting bourgeois considerations before political principles, the non-Communists reiterating their opposition to pointless self-sacrifice. Gray didn't even bestir himself to see them to the door.

My heart went out to him. "Oh, Gray," I said, going over and resting my head on his shoulder. I was uneasy leaving him in his black mood, but I had to get going. My fellow midsummer-nighters and I planned to meet at the studio in Notting Hill a few hours before the performance, to put on our costumes and rehearse a sticky scene or two. Geoffrey was off at some literary function and wouldn't be back for hours. I considered extracting a promise from Gray to attend the performance in Kensington Gardens. He'd have come out of loyalty to me, I was pretty sure, but it didn't seem fair to drag him out at midnight for a mediocre rendition of Shakespeare. In the end, I just kissed him on the cheek and wished him good night.

"Good night, Cara," he said. My face must have conveyed something of the concern I was feeling. "Don't worry. I won't do anything stupid."

I was wrong about Geoffrey and Martin and where they'd gone. Martin had taken Geoffrey to his club, where they'd breakfasted and sobered up, not to mention cleaned up considerably. Gray and I were just finishing our own breakfast when they returned—hale and hearty, as the British say—and ready for a midsummer's adventure.

"Feeling better now?" Geoffrey inquired solicitously, as if I, not he, had been the worse for wear some hours earlier. He trailed me into the kitchen and stood watching as I opened cabinets and checked the contents of our small refrigerator. "What are you doing?"

"Making a shopping list. We've run out of food for dinner."

"Oh, we won't be dining at home tonight," bellowed Martin from the sitting room. "We're going down to Bath."

I looked at Geoffrey, who wore a noncommittal expression on his face. "I was about to ask if you'd like to join us. Martin says the Roman ruins are not to be missed."

"Will you come too?" I asked Gray. He was still in a funk, and had barely glanced at his newspaper. Perhaps the outing would do him good.

Bath was not the magnificent place our host remembered. The city had been bombed heavily during the war, entire streets reduced to rubble, and restoration was barely underway. Martin was particularly distraught over the destruction of the Assembly Rooms.

"*Quel domage,*" he said mournfully. On the drive from London, he'd entertained us with stories of his time in French North Africa, mornings spent swimming in the Mediterranean, evenings parked in a café along the seaside boulevard watching the sun sink below the palms while sipping an aperitif. But he'd grown quiet as we approached the city. Even glimpsed fleetingly from the backseat of his four-seat Morgan roadster, the extent of the damage was striking. I began to understand why he'd spent so little time in England since the war.

The baths themselves were intact, or perhaps I should say that the excavated ruins were largely as Martin remembered them. We lingered on the terrace overlooking the Great Bath, contemplating the history of the place, its sacred origins. From Celtic times, the waters here were thought to arise from a divine source, he told us. The Romans had built a temple beside the spring dedicated to Sulis Minerva, a conjunction of the Celts' goddess and their own. Offerings were thrown into the spring, not only coins, grateful prayers of thanks, but curses too. Vengeful wishes inscribed on lead or bronze tablets, preserved for all eternity.

I think I was expecting something tamer, the mystery kept at a safe distance, behind glass, as it were. Even with scores of other tourists milling about, the place was eerie. Was it something to do with the pale green light of those subterranean chambers, the clammy air, the sulfurous smell of the spa's thermal waters that elicited the primal urge for revenge?

"This is creepy," I said to Gray when Geoffrey and Martin had wandered off to look more closely at some detail of the stonework. "Like being in hell, but with water instead of fire."

My brother, however, was fascinated by the site and seemed untroubled by the evil miasma it gave off. "Ancient spirits," he murmured. "Older than Jupiter and the rest of them and far more powerful."

"What?"

"This place was hallowed long before the Romans came."

I felt a tremor of foreboding. "Damned, you mean."

"Why do you say that, Cara?"

"I don't know. It's just . . . unsettling."

"She's not mistaken," said Geoffrey, rejoining us under the glass-domed roof of the east baths. "There's no telling what dark rituals took place in centuries past. I wouldn't be surprised to learn that the Celts performed blood sacrifices on this very spot."

Gray raised an eyebrow. "Surely not human sacrifices."

"Oh, yes. I'd imagine so. Sacrificing one's fellow creatures is perfectly acceptable when the cause warrants it," Geoffrey blithely assured him.

"You'd know all about that, wouldn't you?" said Gray, walking away in disgust.

Geoffrey went on with his lecture as if he hadn't heard him. "A site like this one was supposed to mark the passage between the daylight world and the Other World, the realm of the dead. One would want to assuage the deity of such a place."

I went to take a closer look at the bronze head of the goddess, in whose name the sacrifices were carried out. She wore a stern expression beneath her braided crown of hair. She would have been an imposing deity, Sulis Minerva, but not a cruel one. Not terrifying, as the carved gorgon's head mounted on the wall, with its bearded face and snake's tresses, was obviously intended to be. Despite the warmth of the day, I shivered.

A visit to the Georgian Pump Room, with its long, tall windows and potted ferns, helped to dispel my apprehension. A small orchestra was playing chamber music and it was possible to imagine eighteenth-century society women passing back and forth in the elegant salon, surveying one another's attire with a critical eye while gossiping about their marital prospects as they did in Jane Austen's time. At Martin's prompting, Gray and I both sampled a glass of the famous mineral water from the fountain in the center of the room. It tasted vile, like ash and sulfur, and it was hot, not in the least refreshing, its bitter flavor lingering in my mouth through several cups of tea and a Bath bun.

Martin proved to be a generous host. That evening we saw *Pirates of Penzance* at the Theater Royal from a private box. At intermission, a bottle of French champagne was delivered to us in a silver bucket. Martin did the honors, popping the cork in one smooth movement and filling four flutes without spilling a single drop. Gray drained his glass in one swallow and excused himself to stretch his legs. When the curtain went up on the second act, he still hadn't returned.

"Perhaps Gilbert and Sullivan is not to his taste," Martin suggested laconically. It was true that my brother had never been fond of musicals, but something was in the air that midsummer's night. A line from our amateur Shakespeare production came into my head, unbidden:

> "They willfully themselves exile from light,
> "And must for aye consort with black-brow'd
> Night."

I felt sure Gray had been drawn back to the baths, that he'd gone to consort with whatever shades inhabited that unearthly site after dark.

★ ★ ★ ★ ★

He was waiting by the car when we emerged from the theater, lounging against the Morgan's fender like a model in some debonair advertisement. Not for the first time, I was struck by his roguish handsomeness. Gray's mother, a foreign-born beauty, had been all the rage in the early years of the century. Her sultry aura earned her vamp parts in half a dozen silent films—she specialized in playing "the other woman"—and while she never attained the status of Theda Bara, she did win Father's heart, not to mention a sizable divorce settlement when he left her, which she invested shrewdly. Like the Gabor sisters, to whom she was vaguely related, she married many, many times, and never to poor men.

My brother had inherited her good looks and that night, outside the theater, he gave off a smoldering allure I'd never sensed before. People noticed him, women and men alike. And he noticed them back, meeting the gaze of his appraisers with frank interest and holding it long enough to cause the majority of them to avert their eyes. As for the ones who didn't avert their eyes, it was these, or others like them I assumed, whom he began to meet late at night in the kinds of clubs that men like him frequented.

Not long after our Bath excursion, Gray announced that the two of us would be looking for another place to live. We could have stayed in the Soho flat—Geoffrey was leaving to spend the remainder of July at the family estate and Martin himself would soon be off to Biarritz—but my brother wanted privacy. He seemed to have tired of political meetings and grew impatient when blacklisted Hollywood people interrupted him at his work. He'd begun a play—"something different" was all he was willing to divulge. He'd grown so secretive since Bath.

"Let me guess: a philosophical drama?" Geoffrey ventured. "One of those deeply moral affairs the French are so fond of these days?" He and Martin were drinking gin and tonics whereas Gray, entering his third week of sobriety, was drinking tonic without the gin.

"Oh, nothing so ponderous as that, I should hope," said Martin. "We could do with a clever comedy, something in a Noel Coward vein, perhaps?" Gray kept mum.

We ended up in a restored carriage house off Holly Hill, at the foot of Hampstead Heath. It felt as if we were living miles and miles from London, in a village of quaint eighteenth-century houses, its parish church displaying a bust of Keats, who'd lived nearby, its winding lanes full of old bookshops, footpaths giving way to stupendous views of the unkempt heath. All of this, and yet the Northern Line took us into the city in no time at all.

That summer I immersed myself in poetry. While my brother typed furiously away at his mysterious play, I lounged in our small garden with volumes of Keats and Shelley, Lord Byron, Robert and Elizabeth Barrett Browning:

> "So grew my own small life complete,
> "As nature obtained her best of me—
> "One born to love you, sweet!"

I will admit that I was caught up in the romantic history of our new home. Walking the narrow Hampstead streets at dusk, watching the swallows dart beneath the eaves of St. John's church, I imagined myself the object of some consumptive poet's yearning. Too late, alas, our acknowledgment of mutual regard, but in his verse our passion would burn for all eternity. Immortal love: I ached to inspire a work of enduring genius. And yet I should have known that the love I sought could not be had without pain. Beauty and suffering were so closely intertwined in the lives and works of the Romantics. Was it worth the price?

Gray's play opened in the West End in the autumn of 1954. *Out of Place* shocked audiences with its frank depiction of an inter-racial love affair—the first time a black man and a white woman were seen to kiss onstage. Some patrons walked out. Critics either loved it or hated it: "Brave, unflinching, and quietly devastating," wrote M. R. Redmond in the *Manchester Guardian*. "American playwright Gray Walden has brought a fresh voice to the British stage, and a welcome social commentary," agreed his colleague in the *Evening Standard*. The *Times*, on the other hand, found the play's premise "implausible," and denounced the "gratuitous violence" of its denouement, while the *Daily Telegraph* and *Evening Standard* vied with one another in churning out synonyms for "repugnant" to describe the main characters' ill-fated romance.

I was touring with a rep company and couldn't make it back to London for the first night. By the time I managed to catch a performance, some two weeks into the run, it was clear that my brother's play was a hit. Richard Hough in the *Sunday Observer* pronounced *Out of Place* nothing less than "a minor miracle." The play's greatest achievement, in the famous critic's view, was the character of Loren (clearly modeled on Dory), whose "nobility of spirit earned him a place amongst the pantheon of classical heroes."

The review reminded me of Geoffrey's comment, when Gray finally consented to show us the work. Our friend was returning to California and we'd invited him to tea at the house on Holly Hill, to send him off. The day was warm for late September and we were sitting outside on the grass. Bees flitted over the fallen apples from our lone tree in the corner of the garden. Fog watched them with mild interest; she wasn't much of a hunter.

My brother read the play aloud, altering his voice for the different characters and pausing, when necessary, to deliver the stage directions. When he got to the end, where Loren dies, I felt my heart break all over again. All the joy and light had gone out of the world in one irreversible moment. How could you live afterward, I wondered?

"My dear boy, it's obvious," Geoffrey said at last, removing his glasses and rubbing his eyes. "You loved him."

Chapter Five:
Adrian
TAORMINA, SICILY, SPRING 1955

The procession wound through the dark streets ahead of us, a line of black-clothed forms half-illuminated in the flickering torchlight. We could have been in any century; not a trace of the modern world marred that scene of ancient piety. So much of southern Italy felt like this. Feudal, as if time had stopped: in Sicily they still had peasants—they even called them peasants—and they were poor beyond belief.

"Another bloody funeral," Adrian complained, his voice pitched low to prevent the director from hearing. We were all in awe of Luca, impressed by his talent and more than a little afraid of his temper, his fierce dedication to his art.

"Shhh!" Salvatore, the gaffer, hushed us from his station by the Klieg lights. Behind him I noticed a few members of the crew making the *mano fico,* the sign against the evil eye. Or maybe they were just being crude; the gesture was ambiguous. A thumb inserted between two curled fingers meant sex, and everyone knew that Adrian and I were lovers. When we were together, I attracted lewd looks from every male over the age of ten. They didn't dare touch me with him there, and I knew better than to venture out of the *pensione* unescorted. Nice women didn't go anywhere alone in that backward country. Not even in broad daylight.

Adrian's status was enhanced by his evident enjoyment of my sexual favors. *Il gallo inglese,* they called him. The English cock: with his deep blue eyes set off against those black curls—they'd dyed his fair hair dark, to make him look Sicilian—he could have had any girl on the set. Why stop at one? was the obvious question. Among the makeup artists, hairdressers, wardrobe mistresses, and the local women hired as extras, I occupied an enviable, if precarious, position. My rivals would have liked nothing more than to see me cast off, ruined, a discarded plaything. Abandoned to the miserable fate I deserved, preferably following a public shaming.

I had a hard time ignoring the ill will of the women around me, and thanks to my boarding school education, I understood enough Italian to pick up on their muttered insults. It didn't take much to imagine myself in the role of spurned lover, either; all I had to do was to look at Francesca, Luca's long-time mistress. Still beautiful and not yet forty, she played the widowed mother of Adrian's character in the picture, a minor role that left her idle for hours on end. Wraithlike, she haunted the set. When she wandered near the crew in her widow's weeds, they'd make the sign in earnest. *La comacchia,* they called her. The crow.

"Luca, you need to eat. Nobody can work the way you do without food." Francesca's voice carried over the sound of the ringing church bells. We could hear Luca attempting to placate her in the gentle tones you'd use with a spoiled child.

"We're filming now, *amore.*"

"Let me make you a plate of spaghetti with onions and anchovies. Remember the spaghetti we ate in Venice? I know how to fix it just the way you like it."

"Later, *amore.* Go back to the villa and wait for me. I will have someone bring you home."

"Ah, no. I will wait for you here."

"*Va bene.*" We heard him sigh. "Salvatore, find the *signora* a stool."

I will admit, their relationship fascinated me. It seemed so

Italian, the way she'd be mothering him one moment, throwing a tantrum the next. Not that Luca wasn't capable of throwing a magnificent fit when provoked. He had a tempestuous nature— *volcanico,* as the Sicilians would say, and they would know—but with Francesca he showed the patience of a saint. Was he sorry for her, or was it guilt? I wondered. What little I understood of Italian Catholicism suggested the latter. Francesca may have been the acknowledged mistress, but Luca also had a wife, albeit one whose name was rarely mentioned. An unhappy marriage, but an annulment was out of the question. She was, after all, the mother of his children.

No, Luca's outbursts were reserved for the rest of us. Adrian and I tried our hardest to please him. Each morning we arrived promptly on the set, although we were expected well before daybreak (and this after a night of passion that left little time for sleep). We never knew what to expect until the cameras started rolling, when Luca would shout something from behind the scenes, some bit of direction intended to inspire us while still allowing for the genuine emotions of the encounter to emerge naturally, as they would in life.

"You have decided to leave your husband," he would tell me, "but Carlo does not know." And to Adrian (Carlo): "You read the truth in her eyes."

My character, Sylvia, was the innocent young wife of an American businessman who had shady dealings with the Sicilian mafia. Adrian played a mafia flunkey. His job was to keep me occupied and out of the way. Initially he resents this babysitting assignment and treats me with barely veiled contempt, but soon, just like Judy Holliday and William Holden in *Born Yesterday,* we fall in love. The affair is discovered and Carlo is murdered to ensure that the deal goes through. Sylvia goes mad with grief; the final scene is a long shot of me, kneeling over his lifeless body on the beach, oblivious to the waves that lap at the hem of my skirt. The camera pans out farther and you glimpse a dignified figure at the edge of the screen, looking on in silence. Francesca.

What can I say? It's not a great film, but watching my cherished copy recently in dubbed Italian, I was struck by its integrity. Luca captured the spirit of that ancient land, its ravaged beauty as well as the harsh lives of its inhabitants, the peasants and fishermen, Gypsies, prostitutes, carpenters, woodcarvers, bricklayers, and blacksmiths, all plying their trades out of doors. They're visible in every scene, background figures peopling the shadows.

The film itself is mostly shadows. *Stolen Love* was shot in black and white entirely at dawn or dusk, the hours of uncertain light when so much remained hidden. He had a thing for indeterminacy, Luca did. Plot, for him, was irrelevant; what little dialogue there was we improvised on the spot, the script having vanished after the first day of shooting, never to be seen again.

"We don't need a script," he insisted when Adrian complained. "Communicate without words, you understand? Speak what is in your heart."

In this, as in all things, Luca was the polar opposite of a Hollywood director, his way of working as far from Father's as could be, and completely unlike the directors I'd known in my brief career on the British stage. But Gianluca Mirano was a legend in the motion picture world and we'd felt lucky to have been chosen for his English-language debut. His first film, *Napoli '44,* a tale of love and betrayal set against the devastation of the allied assault on southern Italy, included footage of the wartime destruction of Salerno. Audiences cried at the opening, or they walked out because it was simply too stark, too soon. Unbearable and yet absolutely compelling.

Italian critics panned it, but serious filmgoers the world over hailed *Napoli '44* as a work of genius, the harbinger of a new era in cinema. Gray and I had seen it in a London art house with a few of his blacklisted buddies in 1952. By then it was already a classic, but its cult status in no way detracted from its power. I still remember the stunned silence in the theater at the film's end.

"So that's how it was," my brother murmured. Maybe that's when the seed was planted, the unflinching honesty of the Italian's vision opening a new avenue in Gray's creative mind, a new standard for dramatic expression. But his ego was not as strong as Luca's. Only by summoning the dark gods of Bath to help him avenge Dory's death did Gray find the will to impose his own terrible vision upon the world. Of course, such forces, once unleashed, will demand their due. How could I have imagined otherwise?

Adrian and I were on the outs that evening of the funeral procession. We'd had an argument earlier in the day and I was still on edge, sensitive to the slightest show of anger or frustration on his part, desperate to restore the harmony between us. It wasn't my fault; I see that now. He was angry inside, the damage done long before we met, but back then I took his every change of mood as a personal rebuke.

"Another bloody funeral," he said, and I reached up to stroke his face, fingertips grazing the rough stubble from chin to cheekbone. He took my hand in his hand, pressed my fingers into his mouth and began to suck them.

"Later," I whispered, conscious of the crew close by, the jealous women watching from the shadows. In response, he squeezed my ass. Behind us, the men were making their rude gestures, interspersed with words of encouragement.

"*Si, Si. Avanti!*" Go ahead. Take her.

"Shhh!" said Salvatore, and all was quiet. I concentrated on the snaking line of mourners while attempting to regain my poise. The scene brought to mind a line from Siegfried Sassoon:

"I stood with the dead, so forsaken and still:
"When dawn was gray I stood with the dead."

The dead were everywhere in Sicily. Like honored guests, they had a place at every gathering, no matter how festive the occasion. Weddings, births, harvests, Saints' Days—you name it. The dead moved freely among the living, and in the catacombs beneath a monastery in Palermo, the dead held court and the living had no right to intrude. None whatsoever.

Adrian is the one who introduced me to the World War I poets. This was back in England, in the early days of our courtship. Late at night, after the curtain came down on whatever production our small repertory company was putting on—Shaw one night, Shakespeare the next—he'd walk me back to my lodgings. Sometimes we'd ramble in silence, worn out by all the words we'd spoken onstage. But often he'd recite from memory the poems of those doomed young men. I'd never noticed cherry blossoms fall until Adrian made me see them through Edward Thomas's eyes,

"On the old road where all that passed are dead
"Their petals, strewing the grass as for a
    wedding"

What was snow to me, before the poet described it, half-thawed on some wintry field in France? Or birdsong: but innocent noise until Thomas, himself no longer innocent, remembered it in "Adlestrop," one of the very last poems he would write.

My romance with Adrian flourished on tour, in the provincial towns with their rundown theaters where we performed for little more than pocket money. I shared lodgings with Maude Latimore, who played the matron roles. Gertrude to Adrian's Hamlet and Mrs. Warren to my Vivie. She was a bit of a *grande dame,* Maude was, but toward me she behaved like a protective mother hen. This brought an element of subterfuge to my budding love affair, which was not unwelcome. Yearning for Adrian sharpened all my senses and lent my Ophelia an exquisite edge. "Never has vulnerability been plumbed to such depths as with Cara Walden's portrayal of Shakespeare's tragic heroine," asserted the theater columnist in the *Star,* Sheffield's daily newspaper. I still have the review somewhere, filed away with other keepsakes from that time in my life.

Maude tried to warn me off. She called Adrian a rake, or maybe "cad" was the word she used. Not a gentleman, she meant, but I took this as an aspersion on his class, not his character. Adrian was a grammar school boy, a butcher's son left more or less to fend for himself at an early age after his mother died in the Blitz. Someone, somewhere, recognized his talent and encouraged him to apply to the Central School of Speech and Drama. There his looks earned him the role of Viola in *Twelfth Night,* the first of several female parts he would play with distinction. My Ophelia owed a great deal, in fact, to Adrian's intimate understanding of her character. His Hamlet showed no remorse in pushing her away, and seemed to know exactly how much pain he was inflicting upon her fragile ego, just how little it would take to destroy her.

"Stay open," he instructed just before we went on. "The poor girl is utterly lost, you know."

Night after night I did as he told me, plunging into the bottomless well of Ophelia's despair. Adrian, my dearest love, was always there to pull me out, and on our late-night walks he'd salve my battered soul with poetry. He promised that Shakespeare would look after me, if I would only trust him. I trusted Adrian *and* Shakespeare. The bard's words: I trust them still, although it's the sonnets I turn to most often now when I want to invite beauty into my life.

But Shakespeare alone could not have brought me to the shimmering heights of inspiration that I attained with Adrian. In his presence I felt golden, luminous, even when the words we spoke were mundane. The scene in *Mrs. Warren's Profession,* for example, the one in the second act, where Vivie grows impatient with Frank's childishness and sends him packing.

"Off with you," I'd say to Adrian in a cold voice. "Vivvums is not in a humor for petting her little boy this evening."

"How unkind!" Frank, his character, would complain.

Vivie: "Be serious. *I'm* serious."

Frank: "Good. Let us talk learnedly, Miss Warren: do you know that all the most advanced thinkers are agreed that half the diseases of modern civilization are due to starvation of the affections of the young? Now, I—"

Vivie: "You are very tiresome." (Here I would open the door to the dining room.) "Have you room for Frank there? He's complaining of starvation."

Cold-hearted I am in that scene, and cold-hearted I remain through the end of the play. Poor Frank will get no more kisses from his Vivvums, yet even at our characters' most callous, sparks flew between Adrian and me, electrifying the other actors. Maude didn't need to catch us making love in an empty dressing room when we thought we had the theater to ourselves; she and everyone else must have known we were lovers from the charged energy whenever the two of us were together onstage. At times I could feel them hovering nearby, our fellow actors, drawing close to bask in our radiance.

"Be careful." Maude's parting words, spoken *sotto voce* as she kissed me on both cheeks, continental style, prior to boarding her train at the end of the run. She might have been speaking Swahili for all the effect her warning had on me.

"Of course," I said, already miles away from her and the rest of the company. Adrian and I were going to spend a long weekend together in Mumbles, the seaside town in Wales where he'd spent summers as a child. He'd been cast in a production of *She Stoops to Conquer* at the Bristol Old Vic and this would be our last tryst for some time—for several months, as it would turn out. I had nothing lined up, but Gray knew of a couple of parts for young actresses in upcoming London productions and was exerting himself to get me auditions; *Out of Place* was breaking box office records and my brother's name was golden.

I was torn about parting from Adrian. Certainly he'd have no time for me once rehearsals for the Goldsmith play got underway. I couldn't trail around after him like some camp follower. Besotted as I was, the prospect of being nothing more than Adrian's girlfriend was not what I wanted. No, it would be better to pursue my own career, angling all the while for another opportunity to appear alongside him, an actress in my own right. Still, I worried that Adrian would find someone else. He was so handsome, so seductive, and well on his way to being a great actor, whereas I had little to show for myself, beyond the plays we'd done in rep. To tell the truth, I wondered what he saw in me.

I tried asking him once, in Mumbles. We'd spent the better part of the weekend in our hotel room, but on our last afternoon we ventured out with sandwiches and bottles of lemonade to picnic in Bracelet Bay. The day was warm for late September, and Adrian was trying to convince me to go swimming; as a boy, he'd swum as far as the lighthouse on the point, which looked like an awfully long way.

"Why?" I said. Sheltered in the lee of the rocky outcropping bordering the beach, we were sharing a cigarette.

"Why what? Why did we swim it? Because we were all intent on proving our manhood." He took the cigarette out of my hand and crushed it out on the stones. "That's what boys do," he said, turning my face toward his and kissing me. "In case you need any more proof."

Absentmindedly, I kissed him back. I was listening to the clinking sound the stones made as they were pulled back into the ocean by the waves, the rough music of the Mumbles shingle. It had taken courage even to frame the question in my mind—why me? is what I'd wanted to know—and I wouldn't find the wherewithal to pursue it. Not then, not later. Not that it mattered, really. I could have listed dozens of reasons why I'd fallen for Adrian, good reasons, bad reasons, all of them plausible enough on the surface. None got to the core of what happened when he and I met. One minute I was standing on dry land, the next I was swept off to sea. The suddenness took my breath away, but it was so exhilarating, the rush of the tide carrying me along. I didn't realize how far out I'd drifted until I was in Sicily, a world away from the shores I knew and lost, utterly lost.

"Peasants in the doorways of their squalid little houses. Peasants in the fields. Peasants trailing after their priests and flinging themselves on the caskets of their departed loved ones. And now we're off to a bloody peasant wedding?" Adrian kicked the leg of the breakfast table, rattling the china and causing my cappuccino to spill out of its cup and puddle in the saucer. "What does any of this have to do with the story, I'd like to know?"

A few days before, Luca had been invited to dine with a duchess at her palazzo, a magnificent wreck of an estate perched high above the town of Gravà. A cultivated woman, she knew all about his films and quizzed him relentlessly on avant-garde cinema while plying him with homemade delicacies: wines pressed from grapes grown in her vineyards, an antipasto course comprised of vegetables from her gardens, lamb and veal from her own animals, preserved fruits from her orchards, including prickly pears like none he had ever tasted. He found her enchanting, and the duchess must have been equally charmed because she'd issued an invitation to all of us, cast and crew alike, to attend the wedding banquet she was giving for one of her sharecroppers.

Naturally, Luca was keen to shoot the entire spectacle. How often did one get to witness an authentic tradition? Perhaps only in Sicily did a hereditary landowner still honor her obligation to the people who farmed her land.

"Just tell me this," Adrian kept insisting. "What are we supposed to be doing there?"

"Non importa," said Luca. It doesn't matter.

I poured my dearest love a glass of orange juice from the ceramic pitcher on the table and set it in front of him. We both adored the freshly squeezed juice of Sicilian blood oranges.

"He's making a bloody documentary!" Adrian complained, ignoring the juice and biting sullenly into a roll. But his fury was passing, I could tell.

"Non importa," I said in an exaggeratedly poor imitation of an Italian accent and was rewarded with a kiss.

The duchess was sending wagons to bring us to her estate, horse-drawn carts, brightly painted, as was the custom in that region. I looked forward to the ride up the hillside. Luca thought that we might be serenaded along the way by musicians playing traditional instruments: accordion, Jew's harp, pipes, and tambourine. Getting into the spirit of the occasion, he'd given me a native costume to wear, a dark blue velvet bodice over a silk skirt, dark blue stockings and striped leather shoes. I felt like someone else, bedecked with rings on every finger, hoop earrings, and necklaces of coral and gold, my hair loose and wild as a Gypsy's.

"Oh, Madonna mia!" exclaimed one of the crew members, who was helping me into a cart. Sylvia was ordinarily demure, a twinset-and-pearls type of girl. Buttoned-up, even in her love scenes with Carlo, the film being intended for distribution in the United States. What Luca intended, dressing me up like a floozy, will be forever a mystery. The wedding scenes were left on the cutting room floor, and just as well. I couldn't have endured any visual reminders of that afternoon.

I didn't sit with Adrian in the cart on the trip up. I sat next to Donald, the American actor who played my husband in the film. His character was a powerful and forbidding figure, a tycoon who surrounded himself with lesser men, whom he bullied and humiliated for his own entertainment. To be honest, he reminded me of Father, who could be quite a tyrant on the set, although Donald was burlier than Father, with slicked-back hair, whereas Father had a full head of white hair, which was always unkempt. Also unlike Father, whose sexual dalliances were legend in Hollywood, Donald's character was quite the Puritan. The same held true for the real-life Donald, who thoroughly disapproved of my affair with Adrian and wasted no opportunity to let me know how far I deviated from his ideal of American maidenhood. "Like father, like daughter," was his all-too-apparent verdict, which he managed to express without uttering a word—an indication of his talent as an actor, I suppose. Short of renouncing sex for good and entering a convent, I didn't think there was anything I could have done to earn his respect.

Needless to say, Italy was hostile territory to Donald. Everything displeased him: the inefficiency of a country where everything came to a halt in the middle of the day so people could go home for lunch, followed by an afternoon siesta. The barefoot children you saw everywhere, clothed in rags, who

never seemed to attend school. The sound of church bells ringing at all hours of the day and night. The strong aromas of
garlic and cheese, of sweat, of animals and manure and wet
earth. The winding roads we drove in convoys of hired vehicles,
taking switchbacks at heart-stopping velocity, en route to one of
the interior mountain towns Luca'd chosen for its picaresque
qualities. The mountain towns themselves, their streets and
sidewalks paved with volcanic rock, were black and gloomy.
Here the people glared at us, mistrustful of outsiders; even I felt
uncomfortable in those towns, but they really were the exception. For the most part, the Sicilians welcomed us with open
arms.

We three—Adrian, Donald, and I—were the only non-Italians
in the cast. The other actors were staying in an abandoned
monastery that had been resurrected for use as barracks during
the war, sleeping on cots and fending for themselves when it
came to meals and showers. We'd been given very nice rooms at
the little *pensione* in Taormina, although we did share a
bathroom. On nice days when we weren't required to be on
location at the crack of dawn, the proprietress served breakfast
on the terrace overlooking the swimming pool and gardens.
Every morning, Adrian and I faced Donald's disapproval as we
emerged from my bedroom or his, unable to repress our sleepy
smiles, but in the spring sunlight with the almond trees in bloom
and the ripening citrus giving off a sweet fragrance that brought
me back to my happiest days at Walden Lodge, I didn't let it get
to me.

Donald reserved his sternest disapproval for Francesca. In his
eyes she was a seductress, and a house-wrecker to boot.
Fascinating and terrifying in equal measure: a *femme fatale*
whose allure was nevertheless quite powerful.

"I don't get it," I once remarked to Adrian. "He goes out of
his way to avoid her, but when she's in the room he can't take

his eyes off her!"

My lover smiled. "Forbidden fruit," he said. "The only kind worth having."

Dressed that day in my Sicilian finery, I must have exuded the same irresistible aura. My screen husband looked as if he wanted to be anywhere but where he was, sitting across from me in a jostling wagon full of rowdy Italians who were stomping their feet in time with the tarantella being played by the accordionist. And yet I felt a subtle change in the atmosphere between us, an unmistakable *frisson* when our knees touched inadvertently. Every so often I'd catch him out of the corner of my eye, looking at me. I kept my gaze fixed firmly ahead, on Adrian, who was riding in the lead wagon. Most of the women were in that wagon too, I noticed.

Our journey up the hillside was being filmed by a cameraman perched on the trunk of Luca's Alfa Romeo convertible. A new toy, the Alfa drew appreciative attention everywhere we went. In Gravà, our procession was brought to a virtual standstill not by the sight of two horse-drawn wagons full of merry wedding guests and musicians, but by our director's car.

"Luca, be careful!" Francesca screamed from the passenger seat as he careened alongside us, angling to give the cameraman a close-up. "Pay attention to the road!" She was dressed quite glamorously that day, in a pink sheath, high heels, and big sunglasses, her chignon protected from the wind by a silk scarf. Everything about her proclaimed Movie Star, but not even she could compete with a red Giulietta Spider.

The duchess put Francesca even more firmly in her place. She shared Donald's view of adultery, it seemed, holding the woman entirely to blame for the man's transgression. Luca was seated at her right at the head of the table, the guest of honor. Donald, Adrian, and I, along with the other Italian actors, sat a bit farther down, mingling with the families of the bride and groom. Francesca was placed decisively below the salt with the most disreputable-looking of the duchess's employees, who ogled her throughout the meal. Gamely, she accepted their invitations to dance—they all wanted turns with the *bella signora*—but from the lethal looks she directed at the head of the table it was obvious there'd be hell to pay on the way home.

I was sitting between an ill-tempered Adrian and an ill-at-ease Donald, and yet I still managed to enjoy the banquet. Keeping with tradition, we were served a main course of baked pasta with meat sauce, followed by a stupendous array of desserts: amaretti, spumoni, sugared almonds, strawberries and Chantilly cream, cannoli, tarts, beignets, and intricate marzipan candies shaped like flowers, animals, and fruit that were almost too beautiful to eat. Then the grand finale: at a signal from the duchess, a tiered wedding cake with brightly colored icing was carried out on a kind of platform. A burst of doves was released when the bride and groom cut into it, to the delight of all the guests, the children especially, who rushed after the birds as they took flight, chasing the fluttering forms until they could no longer be seen in the sky. The whole thing was magical, like being in a fairy tale. Dressed in my Sicilian costume, I felt like I belonged among these simple, good-hearted people.

"Dance with me," I said to Adrian, pulling him out of his chair and leading him to the patch of mowed field where dozens of people were already dancing. Provocatively, I swayed in front of him, moving my hips to the music the way the women around me were doing. I didn't notice that Luca had left the duchess's side, but there he was, beckoning the cameraman over to film Sylvia dancing alone, watched by an unresponsive Carlo.

"Good, good. We have her now," Luca said, smiling approvingly at me. The rest of the guests had stopped dancing, to gather behind the director and watch the filming, so it was just the two of us standing on the grass in front of the musicians, themselves uncertain whether or not to keep playing. Suddenly self-conscious, I made to leave the field, but Luca hadn't finished shooting.

"Don't stop," he urged the onlookers, pushing the closest ones back toward the dance area and encouraging the musicians to resume their jaunty tunes. "We need you all in the scene." Sharply, he scolded Adrian. "Carlo! Why are you standing there with your hands in your pockets? Dance with Sylvia."

Adrian shook his head. "It's not possible that she'd be here. We wouldn't be here either," he said, indicating the Italian actors interspersed among the laborers. "No duchess would invite the mafia to a wedding."

"Forget the duchess. It's a peasant wedding. Carlo's a peasant, no?"

Adrian held his ground. "What's Sylvia doing at a peasant wedding? An American businessman's wife? He'd never let her out of his sight, especially not dressed like that." Here he jerked his thumb at Donald, still at his place at the banquet table, tucking contentedly into a slice of wedding cake. For once he appeared to be having fun.

"Adriano, you think too much." Luca walked over and draped a fatherly arm around my lover's shoulder. "You need to trust this." He poked a finger at Adrian's chest, aiming for the heart. "You are an Italian peasant boy. You see this lovely girl dancing. You don't stop to ask why she is here. You do what a boy does in this country. You dance with her. Even English butchers' sons dance with the pretty girls, eh?"

Angrily, Adrian pulled away from the director's paternal embrace. "Piss off!" The crowd went silent.

"*Va bene.*" Now Luca was angry too. He pointed to a man in the group of laborers, one of the disreputable sorts who'd been seated below the salt with Francesca. "You, what is your name? Giuseppe? Go ahead, Giuseppe. Dance with the *signorina*. Show this *piccola minchia*"—he'd used the Sicilian word for penis, preceded by the word for small—"show him how we Italian men woo a pretty girl."

I danced with Giuseppe. I danced with a few other swarthy Italian men, and was filmed doing so, all the while keeping tabs on Adrian's whereabouts. At first he stormed around at the edge of the dancing field, scowling. Then he leaned against a tree and watched me dancing with Giuseppe, but that seemed to make him scowl more and he was soon gone, striding away from the gathering in the direction of the duchess's fruit orchards. His exit was greeted with hoots and laughter, cries of *piccola minchia* echoing after him long after he'd disappeared over the ridge and down the hill. As soon as I could get away, I went to find him.

He was standing at the upper edge of the olive groves, looking out over the sloping rows of gnarled trees to the green valley below. My heart quickened at the sight of him; was there any man more handsome? He was wearing a loose linen shirt tucked into a pair of tight-fitting black trousers, which accentuated the narrowness of his hips and the inviting curve of his bottom. I crept up, wanting to run my hands down his taut body, but when I touched his back, Adrian wheeled upon me like some wild creature prepared to defend himself to the death.

"It's okay, it's only me," I said, shaken. The look of pure hatred on his face, the face I knew so well, the hardness in those deep blue eyes. It was all I could do not to turn and run back up the hill to the wedding party, but wasn't he my Adrian, my dearest love? Linking an arm through his, I drew him deeper into the grove, down the lanes formed by the rows of silver-leafed trees. We walked up and down as I listened to Adrian rail against Luca and the movie we were making, the Italian director's spontaneous approach to filmmaking, his inability to stick to the script.

"What script?" I said, trying to defuse his rage with humor, but he was too far into his rant to be so easily distracted. By and large, I agreed with my lover. Adrian was a brilliant stage actor whose talents were being wasted in *Stolen Love*. Without dialogue, the scenes between us fell flat. Soulful looks and the occasional chaste kiss conveyed nothing of the inexorable passion our characters were supposed to feel for one another, let alone the passion that Adrian and I actually did feel. It took effort not to kiss and touch when the cameras were rolling with the same abandon we exhibited when they weren't.

Worse still, long segments of the film were devoted to the landscape, random scenes of peasant activities (as Adrian rightly noted) detracting from the drama between the major characters. There was no plot. Everything was improvised. But at the end of the day, who cared? The film wasn't intended for mass distribution. It would play in a few art houses and then disappear, leaving no stain on either of our careers. For now, we were together in paradise, and that was enough for me. Italy and Adrian gave me back the joy I'd lost when Vivien died, the joy I'd felt singing in London, or while listening to Dory and his calypso band.

"I ought to have listened to Richard," Adrian was saying. "He told me I was making an awful mistake, signing onto this project. I remember his words clear as day, when I asked to be released from my contract at the Old Vic: 'In a film you're just a puppet. On stage you're the boss.' That's what he said, and he was right, dammit."

"Surely it hasn't all been awful," I ventured, putting a hand on my hip and tossing my hair so that it fell over one eye, Veronica Lake style.

Relenting slightly, he kissed me on the tip of my nose. "No, Cara. The time we've spent in bed hasn't been too awful."

"Not too awful?" I slapped him playfully on the arm. "You

are an Italian peasant boy. If you want to get the pretty girl into
your bed, you need to do better than that."

Something snapped. Adrian, my dearest love, who used to
recite poetry to me late at night on our walks back from the
theater—that Adrian vanished. In his place stood a man who
didn't care for me at all. And yet he was still beautiful, this
other Adrian who was kissing me now, more urgently, on the
mouth. I closed my eyes and allowed myself to be kissed and
touched, melting as his hand stroked my breasts through the
tight-fitting velvet bodice of the Sicilian dress while our tongues
played, teasing, thrusting. Beneath his fingers my nipples grew
hard.

"Oh, yes," he said. Roughly, he pulled at the bodice, yanking
it down to my waist. I struggled to cover myself back up, but he
brushed my hands away and unhooked my bra, not bothering
to remove it before bending down to suck my breast.

"Adrian! Not here!" We were too public, too exposed out
there in the olive grove. I think I sensed them before I heard the
appreciative whistles, before I turned at the sound and saw the
crowd of men silhouetted against the ridge, watching us, but of
course Adrian already knew they were there.

"What's wrong with you? Adrian, no!" I tried pushing him
away while attempting once more to cover my naked breasts,
but he ignored my protests, shoving me backward up the slope
until my knees buckled and I lay sprawled flat on my back, the
full skirt with its layers of petticoats riding up above my knees. I
rolled to get away from him but was hampered by the petticoats,
and Adrian was too quick, too determined. All I managed to do
was to scratch his face, which served only to enrage him further.

"Bitch!" He slapped me so hard it made my ears ring. Crying, I begged him to leave me alone, but he was straddling me,
fumbling with his belt buckle, unzipping his pants. The next
minute he had me pinned, his full weight upon me, stifling my

protests by pressing his mouth hard against mine and thrusting his tongue inside. With one hand he grabbed my wrists and trapped them above my head. I was writhing beneath him but unable to resist as he tore at my stockings and panties, forcing my legs apart and pushing my skirts up higher. Even as I tried to keep him from entering me, I realized that I was aroused. This was my lover, Adrian, who'd stirred me so many times, in every way imaginable. There was no tenderness in our coupling now, no trust, but my body knew his and responded passionately, as it always did.

He left me there, lying violated on the ground. I didn't notice when he went because I was weeping, and then I must have lost track of time because it was dark when Francesca found me in the olive grove, curled in a ball and shivering uncontrollably.

"Poor child," she said, crouching down and wrapping me in a soft shawl. Someone was standing nearby holding a flashlight, but shining its beam at the ground to avoid blinding us. Whomever it was remained at a polite distance as Francesca helped me to my feet, brushing the leaves and twigs out of my hair and adjusting my clothing as best she could, attempting to make me presentable.

"Is she okay?" said a familiar American voice. Donald, the last person I wanted to see under the circumstances.

"Yes, I think so," Francesca replied. "You are okay, *poverina?*"

I nodded, not trusting myself to speak. What an unlikely alliance, and all on account of me. The two of them seemed incredibly attuned, rescuing poor Cara taking on the importance of a sacred mission. It was as if we'd all entered another movie, something sweeter and more straightforward than the one we'd been in, certainly. This one had a plot.

"The brute!" Francesca said as we entered Donald's circle of light, noticing the smears of blood on my hands and face, the bruise on my cheek. "Look what he did to her!"

They each took an arm, to steady me—I was still shivering under the shawl—as we climbed up the hill and walked back to the duchess's palazzo. The duchess herself was not in evidence, but as Donald was assisting Francesca and me into the backseat of a waiting car, I glimpsed some of the actress's companions from the banquet, possibly including Giuseppe. I tried not to look at the men, I was so ashamed of the scene they'd witnessed. I felt like a whore.

CHAPTER SIX:
STOLEN LOVE

Sunlight sparkling off the water in the bay of Mazzarò, fishing boats moored in the harbor. Ceramic planters filled with fragrant jasmine rimming the balcony where I reclined, on a chaise longue beneath a yellow and red striped awning, like some convalescent passenger on an ocean voyage. There were servants—two sisters who slept in a room off the kitchen. Maria and Caterina. Between them, they managed to do all the housework, but during the initial portion of my stay at the villa, Francesca tended to me with her own hands.

"Chamomile tea," she'd say, setting a tisane on the table beside me. I'd take a sip of the straw-colored liquid, which she'd sweetened with honey to bring out its apple-like taste.

"Thank you," I'd murmur, eyes filling with tears. Even the smallest act of kindness made me cry. "How could he . . ." I'd begin, unable to prevent the tears from flowing.

Francesca would gently wipe them away with the palm of her hand. "Forget him. You are still young, *carissima*. You will love again." *Carissima*. Dearest.

Francesca and Donald had taken turns narrating the story of my rescue on the drive back to Taormina. The wagons had left hours before dusk, without Adrian or me on board. People assumed we'd gone off somewhere together; we'd been known to wander away from the company on occasion. But then Adrian turned up at the *pensione* with a scratched face, ignorant—"or so he claimed," said Donald—of my whereabouts, which

84

awakened the American's chivalrous impulses. Borrowing our proprietress's car, he'd driven directly to the villa where Luca and Francesca were staying. The director was out scouting locations for the next day's shoot, but Francesca had insisted in coming along. She'd been quite frantic about my welfare, urging Donald to drive *con brio*, which he did with great skill, she told me in all seriousness, like an American hero. John Wayne, she called him, which made us both laugh.

On the ride up, they'd evidently discussed my background in great detail. Donald had worked on a picture of Father's years ago. He'd even visited Walden Lodge. ("You were still in diapers; you wouldn't remember me," he offered from behind the wheel.) He'd met Vivien too, and when Francesca learned from Donald how my mother had died, she'd immediately proclaimed herself my second mother. She wouldn't hear of me going back to the *pensione* after the treatment I'd suffered at the hands of that brute, she told me now. I was to stay with her and Luca at their villa, where she'd look after me as if I were her own daughter. Did I know she'd always wanted a daughter? God had not blessed her with children, not when she was married to her first husband and not with Luca, although she'd tried. Heaven knows, she'd done everything to conceive, lighting novena candles to the Angel Gabriel and laying white flowers before his statue in Rome, consulting fortune-tellers and faith-healers here on the island. Everything.

This last bit, about her desire to conceive Luca's child, Francesca had confided to me in Italian in a near-whisper in the backseat of the car, sensing that Donald might not approve. Moved by her confidence, and still upset by my ordeal, I was tempted to tell her the story of giving up my own son at seventeen. I felt sure she'd understand, as my mother would have; at that moment I missed Vivien terribly. Away from Gray and shattered after Adrian's assault, I needed a mother's caring attention so badly. Francesca's promise to look after me was like a wish come true. Gratefully I'd leaned my head upon her willing shoulder and was soothed to sleep as she stroked my hair.

True to her word, Francesca treated me like a daughter, and like a good Italian matriarch, her first priority was to see me properly turned out. "We must buy you some decent clothes. You have nothing suitable for Taormina."

My attire was a matter of great concern to all the women of the household. After dropping us off at the villa, Donald had taken it upon himself to gather together my belongings from the *pensione* so as to spare me any further contact with Adrian. By the time I awoke the next morning, Maria and Caterina had already unpacked my things and were fretting over the paltriness of my wardrobe.

My British clothing did look drab and dated, compared to the stylishly dressed women in Francesca's fashion magazines. Taormina was quite an elegant place, too. In a few weeks, the town would be hosting an international film festival, which Donald and I would be attending as Luca's guests. The rest of the cast and crew would be gone; production on *Stolen Love* was wrapping up and, fortunately for me, few of the scenes that remained to be shot required Sylvia. Only the final sequence, where I learn of Carlo's death and go tearing down to the beach to fling myself on his lifeless body and weep. I didn't relish the thought of being so close to Adrian, but at least there would be no need to pretend I was anything but distraught. Which I was. In spades.

I couldn't stop reliving the assault. I saw myself struggling against Adrian and felt violated all over again, violated not only in the physical sense, but betrayed to the core of my being. My mind kept trying to reconcile the Adrian I loved, the man who'd awakened me to joy and passion, with the monster who'd hurt and humiliated me in front of the others. Those nights of poetry, his lovely voice reciting lines conveying the awe and tragedy of war as we walked through the quiet streets of one provincial town or another, not caring where we went or how late the hour, oblivious to everything but one another. Did I make them up?

But brooding soon gave way to the daily round of life at the villa. Donald had become a frequent visitor. He'd show up for lunch—the big meal of the day, when even Luca put aside his directorial preoccupations and sat down over a plate of pasta—and more often than not, there'd be other guests as well, Italian actors and directors descending upon Taormina in advance of the film festival and journalist friends of Luca's from his school days.

Francesca was in her element, presiding over the table with great charm, ensuring that nobody was neglected, flattering the men with her attention while still managing to endear herself to the women. I marveled at the effortless way she kept the conversation flowing, her skill at eliciting an amusing story from the dour producer who had not once opened his mouth during the first course except to shovel in forkfuls of Caterina's saffron risotto. Her graciousness with the fussy wife of a famous actor who had a delicate constitution and could only digest consommé and champagne. Expensive French champagne and just perhaps, if it was not too much trouble, a spoonful of Beluga caviar.

The gatherings brought me back to the days when my mother presided over my father's dinner parties at Walden Lodge, with Donald standing in for Gray as the semi-regular member of the household, although there was nobody remotely like Geoffrey among the visiting journalists and film people. Really, I'd never questioned his role in all those years. He'd been living in his little cabin at the lodge for as long as I could remember, vaguely involved in Father's film projects, but I never knew what he *did* exactly. Mostly he seemed to muse on the arcane aspects of the productions, suggesting a period detail for the set of some nineteenth-century costume drama, a line of Greek for the dialogue, but I suspected that Father kept him around because he lent an erudite tone to social occasions.

I noticed other differences between Father's gatherings and Luca's. Francesca seemed content to play the hostess, demanding no share of the limelight, whereas my mother had always been the center of attention, even when the occasion was the opening of one of Father's pictures in which she had not starred. She was the reigning monarch and he was more like her consort, watching admiringly from the sidelines as she moved among her subjects, captivating them all. In fact, looking back it occurred to me that Father may have been no more secure in his position as Vivien's husband than Francesca was as Luca's mistress.

Donald's behavior remained as it had been on the night of the rescue. Toward Francesca he assumed a courtly attitude, respectful but remote, seeing as how she belonged to someone else. With me he assumed the role of protector; under his watchful gaze I felt myself reverting back to early adolescence, a good girl once more, but one whose wayward inclinations were not to be tested. This might have annoyed me if I'd been looking to replace Adrian with one of Luca's guests, several of whom (being male, and Italian) eyed me over, but I needed time to nurse my wounds and besides, I'd learned my lesson in regard to older men from Taylor. So I was grateful for Donald's guard-dog tendencies and tried my best to live up to his moral standards, sneaking off to smoke in private when he was writing to his mother, which he did every day without fail.

If the luncheon parties at the villa put me in mind of my parents' gatherings at the lodge, the conversation around the table made me feel like I was back in Martin's flat with Gray and the comrades. Luca was a Communist, as were many of his friends, openly critical of capitalism in general and America in particular. "Coca-Cola," they'd sneer. One sip, their tone implied, and you'd turn all crass and commercial. Their anti-Americanism didn't bother me (I was used to it), but I could tell it made Donald uncomfortable. He'd served with Patton's Seventh Army and still wore his Ike jacket sometimes, complete with rank and unit patches. He never talked about the war in front of me, but Francesca had somehow learned that the blue and silver badge above his name tag meant that he'd seen serious action. She herself was not political. The men could posture all they wanted, her behavior implied, but her function was to be a good hostess. Diplomatically, she'd steer the conversation away from politics and around to safer subjects; the upcoming film festival generally served to distract the gang from their America-bashing.

Actually, this maneuver was also quite familiar from the period of my "confinement," when Gray's frustration over his inability to get work made him something of a loose cannon whenever Father entertained his business associates at the lodge. Our Japanese houseboy was always on hand to escort my brother upstairs before he went too far, but he often managed to get in a few good digs at the expense of some studio boss or producer before Jobo stepped in.

Francesca's strategies to keep Luca's friends from baiting Donald reminded me of Father's frantic efforts to defuse one of Gray's insults after the damage had already been done. I once overheard an exchange between Father and some Hollywood mucky-muck whose ruffled feathers he was attempting to smooth, without success, after one of my brother's sallies. Walden Lodge, in this man's view, was akin to an outpost of the Soviet Union.

"I don't blame Vivien. Your poor wife couldn't help the company she kept. She was surrounded by Reds here, wasn't she, between your son and that British author you're so fond of?" The man had been drinking—he was in no better shape than Gray, really—and his voice was brash and ugly, whereas Father's rejoinder was too quiet for me to hear.

Afterward, when the guests had gone and I was free to venture downstairs, I sought him out in his study. He looked up, startled, on the verge of reprimanding whomever it was who'd dare to intrude upon his privacy, but his gaze softened when he realized it was me. He used to keep a photo of my mother on his desk, not one of her publicity shots—I had an album full of those, from every picture she starred in, along with a shoebox full of postcards she's sent to me while away on location—but one he'd taken on his yacht, when they'd gone fishing off Catalina Island. I love that photo. My mother's hair is blowing off her forehead and away from her face, and the only makeup she's wearing is lipstick, so you see how beautiful she was.

Father beckoned me over to where he was sitting, behind the desk and in front of the photo. I was something like eight months pregnant at the time, and moving around the cluttered room without knocking over one of the towering piles of scripts littering the floor was not easy.

"I remember when your mother was pregnant with you," he said as he watched me approach, a rueful expression on his face. "She wasn't much older than you are now, but she was such a lovely creature, so talented. When she told me she was carrying my child, I vowed that I'd take care of her, always." Here his voice broke, and a deep sigh escaped his lips.

I bent to kiss the top of his disheveled head. Taylor'd wanted to have nothing more to do with me when he'd learned I was pregnant. "You really loved her," I said.

My father sighed again and the saddest expression I'd ever seen came into his eyes. "Love isn't always enough, Carissa."

Luca put off shooting the final scenes as long as he could, but the day came when he could wait no longer. This was it, the tragic ending. Sylvia's heartbreaking reunion with her dead lover.

"I will be nearby," Francesca reassured me. In her black dress and shawl, hair pulled back into a severe bun, she was a forbidding sight. I did feel safer with her around, and of course there was the ever-vigilant Donald, who'd already offered to punch Adrian if he so much as winked at me during our scene together.

"He'll be fine as long as he remembers to stay dead," he said with grim resolve. Standing tall in his Ike jacket, he conveyed the tired heroism of John Wayne in *Sands of Iwo Jima*. Not for the first time since getting to know him, I wondered what had possessed him to make this picture. He deserved better, Donald did. Why wasn't he more in demand, back home? And why wasn't he married, at his age? He had to be in his mid-forties and was quite handsome in his rugged American way. I was sure he'd been presented with "opportunities" galore in the three months we'd been in Sicily. I didn't think he was homosexual; he noticed women, all right, but kept himself apart, as if he'd taken a vow of celibacy. Maybe he was a Catholic, and being in Italy was having a chilling effect on his libido, although it seemed to have quite the opposite effect on Italian men.

I'd been instructed to stay by the lights with Salvatore, away from the other actors, until the actual moment when my presence was required in front of the cameras. This turned out to be a mixed blessing as it provided me with a perfect vantage point from which to observe Adrian flirting with other women. One in particular, a blonde, seemed to be the current recipient of his sexual favors, judging from the proprietary way she kept touching his arm, as if to draw his attention to some aspect of the scenery. We were filming on the beach, the very beach I could see from my chaise longue on the villa's balcony, and I'm sure I was not imagining the sly look he offered in return. A look that implied intimacies shared and promising more to come. How well I knew that look!

The camera crew was busy getting establishing shots of Isola Bella as we all waited for low tide. The island was connected to the beach by a narrow stretch of sand, but the path was submerged at high tide. The idea was that Carlo's body would be revealed as the tide went out. They'd made a dummy, dressed it in Carlo's clothes, weighed it down with rocks and sunk it on the strand. You could just make out a dark patch in the clear water where it lay and the first scene is just seeing the body emerge as the water recedes, with nobody there to observe it. Then a few fishermen come by, nets draped across their shoulders as though they're setting out on their day's expedition. One of them notices the body and they drop their nets and rush over for a closer look.

The next scene (which we'd shot months earlier, when we were doing interiors) is of Sylvia in the hotel suite she shares with her businessman husband. I'm alone, pacing the room, anxious because I haven't heard from Carlo—we've planned to run off together. I've packed a small suitcase, from which I extract an expensive-looking necklace, a gift from my husband. I step in front of the mirror and hold the jeweled pendant against my skin, admiring myself in the glass. Then I lay it regretfully on the bureau, next to an envelope that bears my husband's name in my handwriting.

Someone knocks at the door and I rush to open it, expecting my lover, but instead of Carlo, a boy stands nervously in the hallway. He speaks to me in Sicilian dialect. I don't understand. I'm about to close the door in his face, but he pulls an object out of his pocket and thrusts it at me: the gold crucifix Carlo wore around his neck. I shake my head. No. No. I grasp the truth immediately. Close-up: I raise a hand to my eyes, suddenly blinded by tears. The child takes my hand and pulls me down the hallway, urging me to hurry in a mixture of broken English and Italian.

"*Venga, signora.* You come. *Presto.*"

Now I'm alone on the beach, stumbling toward the body on the strand. I pause to kick off my shoes, leave them behind. I'm running, shouting Carlo's name, kneeling by his body and stroking his beloved face. "Carlo, Carlo." Tenderly I repeat his name as if willing him to awaken from sleep. Then I collapse, sobbing, against his chest. Shift to an overhead shot of the two of us, then the camera pans out, to bring Francesca into the scene.

"*Bravissima!*" shouted our director. "Cut." The best thing about working with Luca was his decisiveness. He put tremendous effort into planning shots, choosing locations, getting precisely the light he wanted, but once the cameras were rolling, he insisted on doing scenes in one take. Sure, he'd shape the raw material into the finished product, poring over the footage he'd gathered, editing out the bits that didn't work, distilling the sequence to its very essence, but he'd never reshoot a scene to get the effect he wanted after the fact. Some artists are like Michelangelo, believing that the perfect statue is already there, in the block of marble, waiting for the sculptor to chisel away the extraneous bits and reveal it. This was Luca's working style: he'd go with what was there, what he had in the can, as opposed to constructing the film in accord with some abstract vision in his head. The director, he liked to say, was as attached to the *real* as sweat was to skin.

I was still on my knees, still Sylvia grieving over her murdered lover, when the cameras stopped and Adrian opened his eyes. His hair was wet, his face made up to look bruised, clothing torn to show he'd been in a fight. Despite all this, he was so handsome it hurt to look at him. I was too open, too vulnerable; when I'd laid my head on his chest and breathed in his smell, I'd felt as if he were still mine.

"Cara." He said my name softly, in a whisper, almost. I think he was asking for my forgiveness. I'm almost sure of it now, but at the time I was having difficulty disentangling myself from the scene, so caught up was I in the grief and loss of our tragic reunion. Adrian was dead to me.

Would it have made a difference if I'd answered him when he called my name? I've asked myself this question countless times, but I'll never know. I got shakily to my feet and walked away.

Not long ago, I saw Adrian in a production of *Richard III* at the Barbican. He'd gone on to greatness, as I knew he would, and although I'd seen him in a number of films over the years, I'd never seen him in a role that appeared to capture his nature exactly as it had crystallized in my memory:

> "My conscience hath a thousand several tongues,
> "And every tongue brings in a several tale,
> "And every tale condemns me for a villain."

And yet, strange as it may seem, hearing Richard's unapologetic avowal of his evil heart, Shakespeare's soliloquy delivered in Adrian's sonorous voice, its tones every bit as stirring as I remembered, I had an insight into the troubled young man I'd loved.

Acting was the only thing Adrian trusted. The theater brought him to life as nothing else could, and he threw himself into his roles with passion and dedication. His gift, his ability to inhabit a character, to imbue a playwright's lines with feeling and significance, carried him far, far away from his tragic past. He became someone else on stage, maybe a collection of someone elses—I'm not sure I got to the bottom of Adrian—but I loved the person he was when we were together, and I liked the person I became when I was with him.

Working in Sicily threw Adrian off balance. Parts of the island had been devastated by the war, other parts destroyed by earthquakes and volcanoes; it was hard to tell what had caused the damage we saw, it was so pervasive. And the people: I'd never witnessed such dire poverty. Entire families living in one room, a cave practically, with a dirt floor and no indoor plumbing, all of them sleeping in the same bed and cooking over an open fire. You'd see scrawny children, hair matted, arms and legs encrusted with scabs. Six-year-olds caring for infants while their parents worked, and still there was not enough to eat and they ran around barefoot, clothed in filthy rags.

That's what bothered Adrian. Not filming amid the desolation *per se*, but Luca's insistence that we delve into the emotion this inspired—our inner devastation, if you will. A more sensitive director could have gotten what he wanted while still allowing us some private space, some dignity, but Luca was pretty cavalier when it came to respecting the feelings of others. He was an *artiste* and his needs came first, an attitude he displayed both on the set and off.

One evening we were shooting a scene in Agrigento. Carlo has taken Sylvia to see the Greek ruins at dusk. The allies had bombed the city to smithereens during the war, but they'd spared the Valley of the Temples, a magnificent set of archeological remains spread out across a ridge below the town. You can't tell from the movie since we shot in black and white, but the stones turn pink at sunset. Our characters share their first kiss bathed in rose light, the setting sun glimpsed through the Doric columns of the Temple of Concordia. Breathtaking: the scene, not to mention the kiss.

Carlo and Sylvia are next observed roaming the streets of the demolished city after dark. Are we looking for a hotel in which to consummate our union, or just too enthralled with one another's company to care about our surroundings? This is one of the many questions the picture leaves unanswered. What you can't help but notice as we pick our way around the rubble are the mangy cats, so many that the very walls seem to move of their own accord—what remained of the walls, I should say. Ten years had passed since the war ended, but the reconstruction of Agrigento had barely begun. To me it was disquieting enough, the shells of buildings and twisted metal of the street lamps, with people actually living in the cellars of those tumbled-down structures, but to Adrian it must have felt like the Blitz all over again. Through the fabric of my coat, I could feel his hand trembling where he held my elbow, guiding me along the sidewalk.

Luca picked up on Adrian's unease and instructed the cameraman to come in for a close-up. "Carlo, are you afraid? This is good. Be afraid."

Carlo's face is half-averted in the film, but even so, you can see his stricken expression. Why didn't I realize what was going on inside him? I knew what Londoners had suffered. Godawful it must have been for Adrian, huddling in the Underground as the bombs fell, hundreds of them in a single night. He'd lost his mother in one of the early raids. He was fifteen and it happened during the day, when he was at school. Their entire block was leveled.

"Not enough light. We can't see that. Salvatore, more light!" Luca shouted. Adrian shook his head and his grip tightened around my elbow. We were moving at a brisk pace, almost too fast for the cameras to keep up. *"Piano, piano,"* said Luca. Slow down.

It's one of the most mystifying sequences of the film. There we are, rushing past a half-destroyed café, past the husk of a post office and the busted storefront of a *tabaccaria*. Carlo is propelling Sylvia forward. He's got his hand on the small of her back and with the other hand he's waving away the onlookers, for people have come out of the basements to watch the couple fleeing.

In fact, Adrian was not trying to clear a path through the crowd, he was trying to get the cameramen to leave him alone. Tears were streaming down his cheeks and his breath came in ragged bursts, as if it hurt to inhale. I so badly wanted to comfort him, to find out what was upsetting him so. Not there, obviously: I waited until we were back in the *pensione*. Alone, finally, in Adrian's room. Passive as a child, he allowed me to undress him and put him to bed. I crawled in beside him and held my lover close. The only thing I could do was to keep him company in his sorrow—perhaps that's all any of us can do for another at such times—but I was twenty-two, and I couldn't bear to see him suffer. With all my heart I wanted to make it all right.

"Talk to me," I urged. "Please tell me what's wrong."

Adrian lay quiet in my arms. His pain was too deep, the grief reawakened by the sight of the bomb-damaged city too overwhelming, to be soothed by my pathetic ministrations. I had my own grief, of course; my loss spoke to his loss. Both of us deprived of our mothers, both vulnerable but putting on a good front, pretending to be strong when inside there was a hollow place that nothing could touch. I loved him more than I'd ever loved anyone in my short life. But it's true, what Father said. Love isn't always enough.

Once shooting ended, Francesca made good on her promise to take me shopping for something stylish enough to wear to the opening of the film festival. We were like two girlfriends on an outing, sharing confidences as we strolled, arm in arm, through

Taormina's chic district, pausing to gaze in the shop windows at the lavish trinkets on display, giggling over some of the season's more outlandish confections. Wide-brimmed hats flat and round as flying saucers. Party dresses with puffed skirts that billowed out like sails.

"Can you imagine wearing that dress on a windy day?" Francesca said, steering me into a boutique in the Corso Umberto. A salesman greeted her by name and ushered us into an elegant showroom. Dresses were displayed on a few racks against the walls—not very many dresses, I was dismayed to see. I was used to shopping in department stores, wandering unescorted through an endless series of rooms crowded with merchandise, pulling clothes off the rack to try on all by myself.

Here, if you were wealthy enough to afford haute couture, shopping was a more refined experience, and if you happened to be in the company of a well-known movie star, perusing the sparse offerings could take all morning. Before we were shown so much as a pair of shoes, we were served coffee. Francesca and the salesman chatted about the upcoming festival as we sipped espresso from petite bone china cups. Our host was deferential, just this side of fawning in his attentions. He had a Don Ameche mustache, which he kept stroking as he listened; once or twice, he glanced at himself in one of the long mirrors and smoothed his hair. Needless to say, he was immaculately attired in a tailored linen suit. Francesca was wearing a stunningly simple sun dress of pale blue silk. Sitting next to them in my flowered shirtwaist (which had looked so stylish in Harrods), I felt frumpy and immature.

Eventually, the conversation worked its way around to the reason for our visit. Francesca explained what we were looking for, and suddenly she became all business. The salesman had brought over a Christian Dior gown in pink Chantilly lace.

"*Signora?*" I might not have been in the room; he addressed himself solely to Francesca.

"Dior," she said dismissively.

"Perhaps this one, then?" He inclined his head toward a manikin displaying a cream-colored *peau-de-soie* evening dress. "It's a Balenciega. All the women are wanting it."

"Balenciega," she repeated, conveying disdain with every syllable. "Why look like everyone else?" Rising from the divan on which we'd been seated, she strode to the rack of evening dresses. In an instant, she'd selected a black silk crepe cocktail dress by a designer I'd never heard of, Arnold Scaasi. "Show her that one, Marco," she said.

"Prego, signora."

I was transformed. The dress had a draped neckline and came to the middle of my calf. Intermission length, they were calling it; with a pair of black stiletto heels and a silk wrap shot through with shimmering threads of gold, I'd be equal to any occasion. And most gratifying of all, Marco noticed me for the first time.

"Molto elegante," he said. *"Ma chi è, questa picciotta?"* Who is this girl, anyhow?

Francesca told him that I was a young actress making her debut in Luca's film, the daughter of a famous American director. *Napoleon and Josephine,* she said, naming one of Father's best-known epics from the 1930s. My mother had played Josephine.

"Ah, *Napoléone e Giuseppina!*" Attentive now, he led me to the rack of daytime dresses and selected a few for me to try on. Naturally, each outfit required the right accessories: handbags, jewelry, shoes. By the time Marco and Francesca had assembled my new wardrobe, we'd spent the equivalent of five thousand dollars! I hadn't brought that much with me to Italy in traveler's cheques. Regretfully, I explained that I couldn't possibly afford so many ensembles. Even if I bought just the Scaasi, I'd have to wire Father for more money to get through the upcoming week of the festival, and once I returned to England I'd be ludicrously overdressed.

Francesca insisted on having my purchases billed to her account. "You must make a grand impression. Everybody will be there."

"It's too much," I protested. "I'm already in your debt."

"This picture will launch your career," she said. "You can repay me later." She pulled a pair of reading glasses from her purse, carefully scrutinized the bill, and signed her name at the bottom. Laden with shopping bags, we left the boutique and made our way back to the villa.

"Yes, I am sure of it," Francesca repeated as we trudged up the via Teatro Greco, the smoking volcano of Mt. Etna framed in the sky above. She gave a bitter laugh. "In another year you will be the famous actress and I will be *una meteora.*" A hasbeen.

That would never happen, I hastened to assure her. People adored her. She had a reputation outside of Italy. Even Americans knew her. We'd stopped at a fancy *gelateria* for granita: lemon ice, delightfully tart, served in crystal bowls. How had I managed to spend three months in this town without tasting a *granita siciliana*?

Francesca patted my cheek. "One day I will come to you for comfort, *carissima*. You will look after me, won't you?"

I didn't take her seriously. What did I have to offer a woman of Francesca's sophistication and stature? "Of course. I'll do anything you ask," I assured her.

Now that he no longer had the film to obsess over, Luca was bored. His boredom took the form of petulance. Around me he was avuncular, as before, and with Donald he was mostly civil (except when the conversation around the table turned to politics), but toward Francesca he began to exhibit a callousness that brought to mind Geoffrey's air of entitlement aboard the *Queen Mary.*

Nothing satisfied him. He found fault with Maria's cleaning and Caterina's cooking, which he blamed on Francesca's lax management of the household. As more and more movie people turned up in Taormina for the festival, he complained that they were wearing on his nerves, showing up at the villa at all hours expecting to be entertained. Francesca tried turning them away, only to be accused of depriving him of company out of a selfish desire to keep him all to herself. Even the rain, which arrived two days before the opening and threatened to ruin the outdoor event, was somehow her fault.

"You'll have your wish," he told her. "So much effort and expense, hopes and dreams, all for nothing."

Francesca winced at the charge, but she did not fight back as she used to do on the set. There were no scenes; she could no longer afford them. The balance of power in the relationship had shifted and it was evident that she now remained at the villa on sufferance, like Scheherazade at the sultan's court in *Arabian Nights,* one of my favorite childhood epics.

Then Donald disappeared. It was rumored that Gina Lollobrigida would be arriving by ship in Palermo and somebody— one of the journalists—had suggested driving to the dock to photograph her when she disembarked. Donald had joined the expedition, but instead of accompanying the others to the harbor, he'd wandered off in a different direction and that was the last anyone saw of him. A phone call to the *pensione* confirmed it: the American actor was gone. The proprietress said that he hadn't returned the night before, although he'd left his things in the room.

We were having breakfast in the kitchen, over the sisters' strenuous protests. In inclement weather, they hung the laundry indoors, on a rack that could be raised high above our heads.

Clearly the kitchen was supposed to be off-limits at such times—the room was steamy with condensation—but Luca said it reminded him of his mother's house and insisted on being served there, at the marble table Caterina used for rolling out pasta.

"Why would he leave so suddenly, without telling anyone?" he wondered aloud, spreading jam on a warm brioche and licking the knife with childlike pleasure.

"We drove him away," snapped Francesca, her natural ebullience returning, and with it the pent-up frustrations of several days. "You with your constant complaining, and always politics. At the lunch table! Couldn't you leave the poor man alone? He fought for Italy, you know. He was right here, in Sicily. Imagine it, the battles, the bloodshed."

Luca interrupted her tirade. "He told you this?" He seemed genuinely astonished by this new piece of information.

"He told me very little. He didn't want to talk about it. Unlike you, Donald is modest about his successes, but it marked him deeply. Anyone could see that!" She threw him an accusing look, put a hand to her forehead, and sighed dramatically. "Ah, it's my fault. I should have protected him." The effect was lost on Luca, however; he was pursuing his own train of thought while absentmindedly chewing his roll.

"In Sicily, you say? But of course, that explains it . . ."

"What does it explain? Your rudeness?"

"Amore," he said, taking her hand and bringing it gallantly to his crumb-laden lips. "You are right. I've been a brute. But listen to me. I know something you do not. I know where we will find Donald. An American soldier can only be in one place. They have a nose for it, and of course their dollars are very welcome."

Mollified, she allowed him to lead her away out of the kitchen and into the salon. "Donald?" I heard her say, before they were out of earshot. At times they treated me like an infant.

Luca left immediately for Palermo. I heard the screech of tires as he went tearing down the hill in the Alfa Romeo, followed by the beeping of his horn, and felt sorry for the terrified pedestrians who'd inadvertently crossed his path. Francesca shook her head and called him a crazy driver, but her tone was indulgent. She refused to tell me where he'd gone, but I gathered it was not in the nicest part of town, wherever it was that Luca expected to find Donald. Throughout the morning, I heard her puzzling it out, talking to herself as she went about her routines.

"I'm sure he had his reasons," she said, arranging calla lilies in a tall vase. "But he must have known he was risking robbery, or worse." She carried the vase to a stand in the front hall and set it down on a lace doily. "Not even in Rome should you go into such places alone. And everything is ten times worse in Sicily."

Tantalizing, these hints, but very worrisome. Notwithstanding his personal code of honor, and the occasional display of male bravado, I had no confidence in Donald's ability to take care of himself in a foreign country where he didn't speak the language. What could have induced a man like him to throw caution to the winds and venture alone into Palermo's most perilous quarters?

Some hours later, I had my answer. Luca returned with Donald in tow, a disheveled Donald with dark circles under his eyes who nevertheless managed to appear happy, almost deliriously so.

"But where have you two been?" Francesca fussed, greeting the two of them at the door and ushering them into the salon, where we'd been half-heartedly attempting to read. She swept a pile of fashion magazines from one of the sofas onto the floor and settled Donald there. Luca she led to the armchair where she'd been sitting. Then she made for the kitchen, where we could hear her clattering around, opening drawers and cabinet doors, issuing instructions to Caterina.

I took up a post by the window, semi-concealed by the drapes, where I could watch both men without drawing attention to myself. Luca wore the smug expression of one who has done a good deed, for which he expects his reward in heaven. Donald was beaming. Each time he tried to assume a more serious expression, the smile would creep back. It occurred to me that I'd never seen him smile that way in the three months we'd worked together. He looked like a mischievous little boy when he smiled.

Francesca returned, bearing a bottle of Marsala and some of the delicious flat cakes that Caterina made from chick pea flour. She served the men first, refilling their small wineglasses several times, insisting that they take more of everything.

"*Carissima,* sit," she said, indicating the chair across from Luca's. I was relieved that she hadn't asked me to leave the room; I was dying to hear the story of Donald's exploits. She brought me a glass of Marsala and a few of Caterina's *panelle*. She herself took the spot on the other end of Donald's sofa, the better to keep his glass filled with the sweet tawny wine.

Luca could restrain himself no longer. Without preamble, he launched into the account of his escapade and all that ensued between finding Donald and bringing him back to the villa. The finding part was not difficult; few Americans wander Palermo's red light district in broad daylight.

"I asked one person, 'Have you seen a big American?' and he sent me to La Normanna." La Normanna was a prostitute known for her vivid red hair, Luca explained. Whether it was really red or came out of a bottle was debatable . . .

"It's real," said Donald, coloring slightly as both Luca and Francesca broke into laughter.

Luca cleared his throat and resumed his story. "*Va bene*. We will take your word for it, my friend. This La Normanna lives in a very small house, and to get there I had to pass through some narrow alleyways where people are living in the streets. They don't have walls, they have curtains, do you understand? Clotheslines hung with rags that separate one family's quarters from another's. I began to wonder how I would ever find Donald here, in this terrible neighborhood. If he were here—how could he be here? Oh, I should like to film this place, show those rich Romans how people really live in this country. Yes, I must come back with a crew and make a picture. It will open their eyes, this picture."

"La Normanna?" Francesca prompted, a touch impatiently.

"La Normanna!" He drank off his glass of wine in one gulp. "What a woman. She lives in the middle of all this poverty, but she is a queen. It is true, Donald, is it not? She is one of them, one of the people, and yet she possesses a force that puts her above them all. Everyone recognizes it, from the smallest child to the oldest woman."

Donald, I observed, did not disagree; it must have been true.

"And there was our Donald, seated like a king in her house, which was a palace compared to the others around it. Very small, as I said, but exquisite."

"Her house has walls," Donald agreed. "And tile floors." I couldn't help but wonder if it had indoor plumbing, but thought it might be impolite to ask.

Luca nodded in assent. "Walls, floors. Rugs on the floors, and not just any rugs. Persian carpets, I'll have you know. And cushions on the ground, as if we were in some Arab tent. Yes, that's what it felt like: a seraglio!" Donald blushed at the comparison, but let it pass. I caught Francesca eyeing him in disbelief, but she dropped her gaze when she noticed me looking. She needn't have bothered; I'm sure my face bore a similar expression. Our difficulty in imagining the morally upright Donald in the lair of some exotic courtesan, however, was nothing compared to our utter shock when Luca resumed the story.

"So, there he was, wearing a robe of silk, reclining on cushions. A sultan."

"Not quite," Donald interjected.

Luca ignored him. "And beside him sat a boy with a face like an angel. Such a boy!" Luca paused in his narration, to heighten the dramatic effect. "Tell them, Donald. Who is he, the lovely boy?"

"My son," he said with quiet pride. "Donatello."

We all stayed up late. Donald told us how he met La Normanna following the Battle of Palermo—which wasn't much of a battle. The real fighting came later, en route to Messina, where Patton's Seventh Army was sent to aid Montgomery's Eighth. Donald was wounded on the second day and was sent to the Evacuation Hospital in Cefalu. There he came down with fever and was very ill. The upshot was that he ended up staying in Palermo, attached to a supply unit, instead of fighting his way to Messina with General Patton. Evidently it was during this time that he and La Normanna became involved. How long the liaison lasted and how it ended, Donald did not say, and his delight over Donatello was so evident that Francesca dared not pose the obvious question.

"But, Luca," I heard her say when he'd returned from taking Donald back to the *pensione*. "How does he know?"

"How does he know what, *amore*?"

"How does he know it's his?"

CHAPTER SEVEN:
LA NORMANNA

Donald insisted in taking us to meet La Normanna the very
next day. It seemed as if he needed to bring witnesses into the
scene, to assure himself it was real. We arrived unan-
nounced—La Normanna had no phone, so there was no way to
let her know we'd be coming—but she welcomed us as if she
had been expecting us, bestowing kisses on Donald and Luca,
clasping Francesca's hands and bringing them to her lips with a
servile little curtsy, embracing me, another representative of her
beloved America, with such gratitude you'd imagine I'd had a
hand in liberating her city from the Nazis.

Francesca did not take to her. The woman was too brash, her
sexual allure as bold as the color scheme in her living room,
which resembled the set of *The Sheik*.

"All we need is Valentino," I mused aloud, earning a smirk
from Francesca. La Normanna filled the room, radiating light
and heat while using up all the air. Here was a creature who
had survived the war and its aftermath through sheer force of
will, a tigress with flaming red hair and a temperament to match.
And yet she possessed a disarming transparency that the
sophisticated Roman actress lacked. She held nothing back,
savored life's pleasures with such zest that you could not help
but enjoy yourself in her company.

Luca was not in thrall to her as Donald seemed to be, but he
was fascinated all the same. A scientist discovering a primitive
form of some familiar species would want to study it closely, the

better to appreciate the more highly evolved version. So it was with the director and La Normanna: everything she said or did intrigued him. A moment after she'd seen to it that we were settled comfortably on cushions on the floor, she disappeared behind a beaded curtain, returning an instant later with a wad of money, which she handed to the boy.

"Donatello, *vai al convento.*" In halting English, she translated the command: "I send him to the good sisters."

"Ah, the nuns." Luca nodded sagely, as if this made perfect sense.

"*Ma, perché?*" Francesca interrupted. Why is she sending him to the nuns? La Normanna explained in a flood of words, a rapid torrent of which I caught only the occasional *lei,* the polite term of address.

Luca summarized in one short sentence for Donald and me. "They make the best cannoli in all of Italy."

Divine cannoli! Donatello returned with a large box of the pastries, enough to feed a gathering many times the size of ours, but we made short work of the flaky ricotta-filled tubes—all of us except for Francesca, who declined the cannoli and the coffee La Normanna served to go along with them. The slight had its desired effect; La Normanna sulked for the rest of the afternoon, pointedly snubbing Francesca while lavishing Luca with attention.

"How can you dislike her, *amore?*" We were back at the villa, just the three of us, Donald having stayed on in Palermo with his "family." He was planning to marry La Normanna and bring her and his son back to the States, make Americans of them. He'd already set to work on the task of improving his fiancée's English while we were there, having her repeat phrases and expressions, quizzing her periodically to see if she was learning. I had the impression that La Normanna's English vocabulary consisted largely of words that didn't bear repeating, not in public, at any rate. Donald had his work cut out for him.

Donatello was a different matter; he was a natural mimic and remembered everything. With his cute face and his quick mind, he'd do fine in America, I had no doubt. There was the matter of his name, of course. He was called Antonio on the street, or just 'Tonio by his friends. Even La Normanna slipped once or twice and referred to him as Antonio, much to Donatello's annoyance.

"Donatello, mama. *Mi chiamo* Donatello."

This was the issue that Francesca raised, in response to Luca's question. "She's a liar. The child isn't even the right age."

I had to agree. Donald's son would have been born in 1944, but 'Tonio was no eleven-year-old. Making allowances for poor nutrition, he was still too small; nine would have been my guess. But Luca saw this as a minor detail.

"She will take care of him in America. A woman like that knows how to make a man happy!" Here he made a hand gesture I'd never seen before, inserting the tip of his nose in a V sign.

Francesca threw up her hands in exasperation. "That's all you men think about."

"Our friend is in heaven. Can you deny it?"

"Sooner or later he'll figure it out," she protested. "He isn't stupid."

"Nor is she, *amore*. La Normanna will give Donald more sons in America. She's fertile."

I believe that everything that happened in Italy from this moment on goes back to those two words: she's fertile. Granted, the trip to the catacombs didn't help. We were looking for a diversion and, given the rain, an outdoor excursion was out of the question. Spending time in Taormina was also out of the question with the film festival due to begin the following day. The town was crawling with celebrities, journalists and hangers-on, the narrow streets jammed with cars and tour buses from other parts of Italy. All in all, a jaunt to Palermo seemed like a good idea, although Luca's impromptu decision to invite Donald and "family" to join us put Francesca in a foul mood.

We hired a private car and driver to take us to Palermo, as we had the day before with Donald, but it was pretty cozy once we'd picked them up, with Francesca sitting between Luca and the driver in the front seat and the rest of us squeezed in the back. Also, La Normanna made us wait for an eternity while she finished her toilette. Luca and the driver had time to smoke several cigarettes apiece before she appeared, dressed in a tight-fitting flowered dress, her red hair pinned up under a smart little hat with a veil—a new gift from Donald, we were told.

"Last year's fashion," Francesca muttered just loud enough for La Normanna to hear.

"Oh, basta ascoltare la cagna vecchia e brutta!" Just listen to the ugly old bitch, retorted La Normanna.

Luca struggled to maintain a civil atmosphere in the car. *"Donne, per favore . . ."* Ladies, please.

Our destination was a good drive from La Normanna's neighborhood. By the time we arrived, everyone in the car was perspiring, and not from the humidity alone. I was wedged between Donald and 'Tonio, who'd brought along a model racing car, his new gift from Donald. Watching him play with the toy, I lowered my estimate of his age to seven or eight. The lack of self-consciousness as he pretended to drive the car along the back of the front seat while making little engine noises, his utter concentration on the game, reminded me of myself at that age. But Luca's verdict was borne out by Donald's fond gaze. He was crazy about the boy—a fact that did not go unnoticed by Francesca.

The catacombs were built beneath a Capuchin monastery on the outskirts of the city. Never could I have imagined such a place! Dried-out dead bodies dressed in their finest attire, the corpses hung from the walls or were displayed in macabre little tableaux. A corridor lined with rows of shriveled monks bowing to the passersby, submissive even in death. Another hallway given over to priests and bishops, among them a number of ladies too well dressed to be housekeepers. Then there were soldiers from any number of wars, a hall for aristocrats, a corridor for doctors, lawyers, judges, family groups and married couples. A separate chapel was devoted to girls and women who died as virgins, a particularly dusty-looking group to my eye.

Some of the corpses were centuries old, little more than skulls and bare bones, hardened skin and clothing hanging off them in tatters. The newer bodies had facial hair, eyebrows, lashes, beards, their desiccated faces displaying a range of expressions. One pair caught my fancy: an elderly couple nailed up in the aristocrats' hall. The wife wore a burgundy dress with a lace collar, her husband a blue suit with matching ascot, velvet waistcoat and eyeglasses. The way they were hung, it appeared as if they'd been caught in the middle of an argument. The wife seemed to have been getting the better end of it; her head was turned, mouth open as if she'd been caught in the middle of a harangue, while the poor man was looking down at his feet. Had they been arranged that way on purpose, enacting in death the behavior they'd shown in life? I tried to imagine their adult children visiting them down here, taking comfort in seeing Mama and Papa still carrying on as usual. If it had been me, though, I'd have allowed Papa to get a word in edgewise.

Luca had paid one of the friars to give us a guided tour. The man took his duties seriously, noting features of the military uniforms—the soldier from the Napoleonic era wearing the French bicorne—and insisting that we linger in front of the more illustrious corpses so he could tell us their stories. He'd saved the best for last: turning a corner, we came upon a chapel dedicated to one little girl, Rosalia Lombardo. She was just two when she died of pneumonia in 1920, the friar told us. The Capuchin brothers had stopped taking bodies in 1871, but her parents begged to have her laid to rest in the catacombs, and an exception was made for Rosalia. There she lay, embalmed in a glass-covered coffin, a discolored sheet tucked right up to her chin. Eyes closed, long eyelashes brushing her cheeks, lips slightly parted, a yellow bow tied in her wavy hair. She could have been asleep. I had to turn away; it was too much. The adults I could handle, but to see an innocent child like Rosalia! A beloved child deprived of life.

"Papa, look!" said 'Tonio, tugging at Donald's sleeve. But Donald too was trying not to look. Ever since we'd entered the place he'd been hanging back, casting furtive glances behind him as if to make certain he knew the way out. While our guide explained the mummification process in grisly detail, and Luca translated with what struck me as unnecessary fidelity, our friend was turning pale.

"Excuse me," he said, putting out a hand to steady himself against the wall. A moment later he'd slumped to the ground.

La Normanna went into hysterics. With a shriek, she threw herself on the stone floor next to Donald's body and twined her arms around his chest while 'Tonio burst into tears.

"Papa!"

Donald's eyes fluttered open. "Donatello." Extricating himself with some difficulty from La Normanna's embrace, he pulled himself into a sitting position against the wall. The boy climbed immediately into his lap, and Donald hugged him tightly. Luca spread his palms and looked at Francesca as if to say, *What did I tell you?* The actress tossed her head in annoyance. Turning on her heel, she left abruptly, heading for the exit. Luca and the guide helped Donald to his feet and we trailed behind in Francesca's wake, but were brought up short at the end of the corridor by the sight of the actress standing stock still, frozen in front of a small chapel that resembled Rosalia's.

I shouldn't have looked. There, stuffed into niches in the walls, were babies, dozens of them. Infant skeletons dressed in embroidered gowns and wearing little bonnets. A small boy was posed in a rocking chair, holding his baby sister in his lap. Nearby, in the foreground of the chamber, stood several infant-sized coffins where the little bodies lay cradled in silk, their heads resting on pillows, hair and clothing lovingly smoothed into place. One baby girl in a flowered dress looked right at us, an expression of curiosity on her face as if she expected us to explain what she was doing among the dead, she whose dried-out features still carried so much of her personality.

"*Carissima.*" Francesca took my arm and drew me to her side. Tears dampened her eyes and at the sight, I felt the agony of my surrendering of my son rise up in me, the return of all the pain and remorse I'd suffered before fleeing with Gray and Geoffrey to England. We'd shared many confidences in our time together at the villa, Francesca and I. She knew about my baby and I knew that she'd suffered several miscarriages, some in her marriage and at least one since she'd been with Luca. Now we both gave in to our sadness in front of the infants' chapel, arms entwined, supporting one another in silent grief for the children we'd lost.

Our guide dropped to his knees and began to pray for the souls of the dear babies. They were with God, he assured us, motioning for us to join him on the cold floor and offer our sorrows to the Lord. La Normanna, 'Tonio, Francesca, and I were quick to comply; after a moment's hesitation, even Donald knelt alongside us. Luca remained on his feet, standing off to the side, arms folded across his chest. Religious displays only interested him when they involved peasants, his stance proclaimed.

★ ★ ★ ★ ★

We emerged from the catacombs into the bright sunlight and sweltering late afternoon heat. Palermo was not a city of tree-lined boulevards. No sidewalk cafés beckoned, no air-conditioned *gelaterie* as in Taormina—not in the vicinity of the monastery at any rate. Luca ushered us back into the waiting car and asked the driver to take us to the Caffè Mazzarà, an elegant pastry shop off Piazza Verdi, the favorite hangout of Palermo's artists and intellectuals. He did seem solicitous toward Francesca in the front seat, draping an arm around her shoulder and pulling her close.

Once we were en route, La Normanna turned her full attention to Donald. Retrieving a handkerchief from her handbag, she moistened it with eau de toilette and attempted to dab at his temples.

"Please, I'm fine," he told her, leaning away from her reach.

"Papa fine," said 'Tonio.

"Papa *is* fine," Donald corrected him gently.

"Papa *is* fine," the child repeated, matching the intonation and earning a glorious smile from Donald. Pushing his advantage, he tried out another phrase. "I have chewing gum now?"

We all laughed; even Francesca softened. "He already sounds like an American," she said.

"Chewing gum and Coca-Cola," Luca promised. *"Va bene?"*

Caffè Mazzarà was famous for its Sicilian pastries and for its coffee *granita* served with fresh cream. Unfortunately, all of Palermo knew it. While we waited for a table to free up in the ground floor bar, Luca scanned the room.

"Amore," he said in a stage whisper, drawing Francesca's attention to a plump gentleman eating a slice of *cassata* not thirty feet from where we were standing. "Isn't that Gigli?"

"Gigli?" Francesca was unable to keep her voice to a whisper.

"Beniamino Gigli!" At the sound of his name, the object of her inquiry looked up from his plate, his expressive face registering surprise, recognition, elation in quick succession. An instant later he had risen from his chair and was beckoning her over with great enthusiasm. Standing up, he wasn't much taller than he'd been sitting down.

"No, no. Don't go! I'm begging you, don't talk to him!" Luca hissed, but it was already too late. Francesca and the little man were greeting one another with kisses and exclamations of joy. We watched as Gigli made an elaborate show of pulling out the actress's chair, seeing to it that she was settled at his table before summoning a waiter—several of whom were hovering in attendance—to take her order.

"If she thinks I'm going over there to pay tribute to that fascist, she'd better think again," the director muttered, but there was Francesca, pointing him out to her companion. Luca slapped his forehead in dismay. Just then a table opened up on the other side of the room. Luca seized on the opportunity, motioning for the rest of us to claim it before someone else did so. La Normanna was quick to follow his orders, dragging 'Tonio along, with Donald and me trailing in their wake. Luca joined us a few minutes later and deliberately seated himself with his back to the other couple. The snub earned a nod of satisfaction from La Normanna, which neither of the men noticed. They had their heads together and Donald was quizzing the director on Gigli. I strained to overhear their conversation against the clamor in the café.

"That's him? *The* Beniamino Gigli? The famous tenor?"

"*Si, si.* Caruso Secondo," said Luca, too flustered from the encounter to realize he was speaking Italian.

"Why don't you like him?" Donald pursued. "I heard him years ago in *La Bohème.* He was fabulous."

"His singing, yes. Fabulous. His politics not so fabulous, I am afraid."

Donald frowned in disapproval. "Does everybody in Italy have to be a Communist these days?"

"My friend, there is much you do not understand about the world." The director's voice grew grave. "I know you fought here, for my country. I believe you are a man of courage, of honor." Here he looked at La Normanna, who smiled back at him coquettishly, despite having not a clue of who or what the two were talking about. Opera did not seem to be one of her interests.

'Tonio returned from surveying the pastries in the front of the room, overwhelmed by the selection. "Papa," he said. "I have two?"

"Donatello, no! Is not polite." La Normanna scolded. Donald, however, was more concerned with correcting the boy's English than with his manners.

"*May* I have two?"

"*May* I have two?" echoed 'Tonio.

"Please," his mother added with a stern look.

"Please, Papa. May I have two?" His smile would have melted even the hardest man's heart. Luca motioned for a waiter, and it wasn't until we had all ordered quantities of pastries and ices that he returned to his earlier subject.

"Gigli sang for Mussolini. He sang a beautiful *Aida* in Munich for Adolf Hitler." Here the director could not keep a bitter edge from his voice. "I am told the Führer gave him an autographed photograph as a token of his appreciation."

Donald let out an exclamation of disgust. "You're kidding!" He turned in his seat to glare at the singer.

Luca shrugged. "It is not something we talk about, you understand. There is much we would prefer not to remember about those dark days in our history, but Italians know. After the war, Gigli was very unpopular. Crowds surrounded his house in Rome and for months he was afraid to go outside."

"Why is Francesca having coffee with him?" I spoke without thinking, regretting the question the instant I saw Luca's scowl.

"Ask her," he said. "I would like very much to hear her answer."

In fact, Francesca answered the question without my prompting. The moment we'd dropped off Donald and the others and were on our way back to Taormina, she launched into a diatribe, berating Luca for his rudeness toward the famous tenor. This, on top of his insensitivity in taking us through the catacombs— both of which paled, however, before his absolute idiocy in inviting La Normanna along on the excursion.

"That woman!" Francesca fumed. "If you dare to put me in the same room with her again, I swear I will not be accountable for my actions."

"Go ahead. Degrade yourself further."

"What do you mean, degrade myself further? I'm not the one who brought that whore out in public. Did you see the way people were looking at her in Mazzarà?"

We'd changed places in the car. I was in front with the driver, the two of them were in the back, arguing so vociferously that I found myself singing "Mairzy Doats" over and over in my head, in an effort to drown them out. The interlude in the café hadn't been enough to counteract my distress over the infant skeletons, and now the argument was stirring up less-than-happy memories of events at Walden Lodge—events I hadn't thought about for years.

Father hadn't approved of Vivien's involvement in left-wing politics. Late at night, I'd hear them arguing, throwing accusations at one another, cruel words that it hurt me to hear because I loved them both. I was too young to understand what they were saying, but lying awake in my bed as they fought, I'd turn snippets over and over in my mind, trying to make sense of them:

"For God's sake, Robbie. I'm not a teenager any longer."

"You're my wife, and we've both got careers and reputations to consider."

"You were prepared to let your son go to Spain."

"I had no control over Gray at that age, as you well know. Fortunately for him, he saw reason before it was too late."

"But you think you can control me, is that it?"

"You've given me no grounds to believe that you'll ever see reason, my dear."

At the time, my sympathies were almost entirely with Father. I'd gotten used to Vivien's absences when she was working on a picture, but when she was between projects I wanted her home, not running out to meetings that lasted all night. Even when she was around, her mind was often elsewhere in those days. And yet she seemed happier, less inclined to find fault than she'd been in the past. More likely to laugh at a moment's notice, for no discernible reason. When we were together, just the two of us, I remember happy times. As a child, I noticed the symptoms without being able to diagnose the malady, but looking back with the eyes of an adult, I could pinpoint the cause easily enough.

She was like me in the early phase of my romance with Adrian. The revelation hit with the force of a blow to the head. I felt dizzy, so disorienting was its effect on my understanding of my parents' marriage. Had my mother fallen in love with another man? The child in me didn't want to believe it, but going back over various details I remembered from that period in my life put a new complexion on Vivien's behavior.

She'd changed: in retrospect, that's the main thing that struck me. Thinking back, I could trace that change back to a specific event. In 1942, she'd gone to Mexico to shoot *Moonlight Fiesta*, one of those frothy, south-of-the-border musicals they were making during the war. Not one of her best pictures by a long shot, but memorable for being her last (she'd been working on a new film with Father, but the production was still in its early days when she drowned, and Father didn't have the heart to make it).

Vivien came back from Mexico intent on self-improvement, beginning with her education. She'd never finished high school, having made her screen debut at fifteen, but Geoffrey was happy to tutor her. I'd find them huddled together over a pile of books when I came home from school, working their way through the classics. At ten, I was no judge of my mother's intellectual ability, but she did impress me as hard-working. Every night, while I sat doing my homework, she'd be reading and taking notes, running out to consult Geoffrey on some matter or other. The two of them were thick as thieves. This went on for several months, and I have the impression that it was Geoffrey who put an end to the sessions. He'd started a new novel and needed the time to write. So Vivien sought instruction elsewhere, in the den of radicals, if the newspapers were to be believed. Or in the arms of one radical, the mystery man she was seen with in the cocktail lounge?

Once the suspicion entered my mind, it took hold and wouldn't let go. If Vivien had been carrying on with another man, who was he and how did they meet? How did they manage to keep their liaison secret? The gossip industry in Hollywood was so persistent; had there been so much as a hint of an illicit romance, you can be sure some columnist would have aired it. And yet, the subject of the mystery man—the last person to see Vivien Grant alive—was never pursued. One question led to another. Even if Vivien and her lover had succeeded in hiding their affair from the press, wouldn't someone have known? The small signs I'd picked up as a child without understanding their significance would not have gone unnoticed by Father. It takes one to know one, as they say; wouldn't he have suspected his wife of cheating, given his own history of adultery?

All of these questions were going through my head as I tried to ignore the argument in the back of the car. We were driving along the island's northern coast, passing rock-strewn fields that sloped down to the sea. To our right mountains loomed, their jagged edges stark against the darkening sky. In another mood, I would have found it all quite beautiful, but now it struck me as ominous. The landscape spoke of violence; it was hard to imagine human warmth or kindness in such a harsh setting. The sum of my experiences in Sicily, the extreme contrast between Taormina's wealth and the dire poverty we encountered everywhere else on the island, the wartime ravages, Adrian's assault, the dried-out bodies in the catacombs—I felt oppressed by all of it, frightened, sad, and very much alone.

Luca and Francesca eventually tired of their argument and we made the remainder of the trip to Taormina in silence. The sisters had left out a cold buffet of cheeses, bread and marinated vegetables on the sideboard in the dining room, but I didn't have much of an appetite and went straight up to my room. The next day was the gala opening of the film festival, but the prospect of making my debut in my sophisticated new dress no longer excited me. I wanted to be back in London with Gray, reading poetry in the garden of our Hampstead cottage with Fog curled in my lap.

CHAPTER EIGHT:
PADRE PIO

"*Carissima,* wake up!"

I opened my eyes. Francesca was perched on the end of my bed, dressed in black, as if preparing to reprise her role in the film.

"What time is it?" I said between yawns.

"The time? Who knows? It doesn't matter. Hurry, *carissima!* We are leaving."

"Leaving?" I sat up and reached for my watch on the bedside table. It was barely six a.m. But why was she wearing black? Had someone died?

"Hurry, hurry!" she urged. Already she'd opened the armoire and was rifling through my clothes, pushing aside my blouses in frustration, evidently unable to find what she was looking for. "Don't you have anything black?"

Joining her at the armoire, I extracted a black crepe skirt. Somewhere among my things was an off-the-shoulder knit top that went with it, although I didn't remember seeing it since I'd left the *pensione.*

"What happened? Is somebody hurt?"

Francesca had turned her attention to my bureau drawers. "Wear this!" she tossed a short-sleeved black cashmere sweater onto the bed. Sylvia's sweater, part of the outfit she was wearing when she got the news about Carlo. There was also a hunter green jacket and matching skirt, although the skirt was somewhat the worse for wear, having gotten saturated with seawater during the shoot. When Maria saw it, she'd pronounced it ruined.

"Please, Francesca. Where are we going?"

"Get dressed and meet me downstairs," she said. "I had a vision, *carissima*. Padre Pio came to me in a dream."

"Padre Pio? Who's Padre Pio?"

"There's no time to explain. Just hurry. I'll tell you everything in the car."

Francesca drove even more recklessly than Luca. *"Imbecille!"* she shouted, waving her fist at the driver of a car she'd narrowly missed on the last hairpin curve. I didn't dare distract her with questions; white-knuckled, I fixed my gaze on the approaching town of Santa Teresa di Riva. I'd just gotten my period, which was a relief, of course. But between the cramps and worrying how far I could make it without leaking all over the Alfa's posh leather seats, our destination was the least of my concerns. *Just get me to a drugstore,* I prayed silently. *A box of tampons and a bottle of aspirin: is this too much to ask?*

Santa Teresa di Riva had a raggedness about it, like so many wartorn towns in Sicily; in the dawn light, with most of the businesses shuttered and only a handful of people on the streets, it felt like the war was still on. Any minute the troops would be marching through: Germans retreating before the Allied advance, or Americans establishing their positions in the newly taken town, still wary of snipers. Then, no doubt, the bombardment would start again.

We parked in front of a massive tower by the bombed railway bridge and made our way on foot to the town center. Two women out in public at that hour could only mean one thing, but Francesca had come prepared. From her satchel she withdrew a black shawl for each of us. I followed her lead and draped mine over my head and shoulders, adjusting it to cover my décolletage, the small amount of skin left exposed by Sylvia's sweater.

"*Brava*. Now we are invisible," Francesca said. We looked like two widows on their way to Mass. Eyes downcast, we kept to the main thoroughfare and were soon rewarded by the sight of the green and white sign of a *Farmacia*. I made my purchases and repaired to the toilet of a nearby café to attend to my personal hygiene. Over cappuccinos, I finally learned the reason for our trip.

"Can you tell me now why we're going to see this Padre fellow?" I asked, trying to keep my voice neutral. Had Francesca dragged me out of bed at this ungodly hour to go to church? It wasn't even Sunday! What's more, we both had hairdresser appointments later in the morning. I wanted to look my best for the opening.

"Padre Pio! Don't tell me you haven't heard of him. He's famous, even in America. He performs miracles."

I couldn't hide my skepticism. "What kinds of miracles?"

"He reads the heart, *carissima*. He sees through to your very soul." People's lives were changed by him, she informed me. An actor she knew, Carlo Campanini, was now his disciple, and there were many others who'd turned their backs on the world and devoted themselves to the good father. They came from every country to see him, and many stayed in San Giovanni Rotondo to help with his work.

"You're telling me that this man, Padre Pio . . ."

"Padre Pio is not a man. He is a saint! A living saint. Do you know that he has the stigmata? When I saw him last night, his hands were bleeding, just like our Lord's. That's how I recognized him."

"If you just saw him last night, why do we need to go to him now?" I'll admit I wasn't in the best of moods. The aspirin had taken the edge off the pain, but I still felt achey and lethargic. I should have been in bed with a hot water bottle, resting up for our big night, not driving around Sicily on some kind of holy mission.

Francesca was also running out of patience. "I told you already. He came to me in a dream. I felt it like a summons." The actress looked at her watch. "Oh, Dio! Finish your coffee. We have a long way to go if we intend to make it in time for evening prayers."

"Wait a minute," I said. The first glimmer of apprehension taking hold in my mind. "What about the film festival?"

"Yes, I'm sorry about that. We won't be back in time for the film festival. San Giovanni Rotondo is not in Sicily, you know. First we must catch the ferry in Messina. Then we'll drive up through Calabria to Puglia, on the Adriatic coast. It is beautiful there. Very peaceful, I'm told."

When I was small, Father used to play this game where he'd dangle me upside-down and tell me to describe the world, just the way I saw it.

"I see trees growing out of the sky, leaves first!"

"Good, good. What else?"

"The lodge is balanced on its chimney. And here comes Jobo, walking upside-down across the lawn." The sight struck me as incredibly funny and I broke into giggles. "The grass is the ceiling and the sky is the floor."

The sound of my laughter made Father laugh too. "The sky is the floor," he repeated, quite taken with the idea. We both lay on the ground and gave full rein to our silliness. Closing my eyes, I imagined myself striding barefoot across the sky, the air cool between my toes. Every so often I'd pause to kick aside a misty cloud as it rolled by.

"I wish I could really walk on the sky," I said.

"Aren't you afraid?"

"Of course not." I wasn't afraid of anything in those days. Vivien's death was still years in the future, Walden Lodge my very own realm where I presided like a fairy-tale princess.

Father got to his feet and brushed himself off. "Brave girl!" he said, offering me a hand. "But you ought to be a little afraid, don't you think?"

"Why?"

"The sky is infinite, Carissa. You might fall in."

Not until we'd boarded the ferry for the mainland did I realize that Luca had not loaned Francesca the car. Apparently he had no idea we'd left.

"I couldn't tell him. Promise me you won't tell him either. He mustn't know we've gone to see Padre Pio." A note of desperation had crept into her voice; she seemed to have an awful lot riding on this expedition. I felt indebted to her for taking care of me; she'd become my best friend and mother surrogate, all rolled into one, but now I felt like the parent.

"Francesca, are you serious? You took Luca's car and you didn't tell him where we're going?" We were standing at the rail of the top deck, watching the island recede as the ferry steamed toward Italy's toe. Francesca had wrapped her shawl more tightly around her head, to protect her coiffure from the salty spray, but I liked the sensation of the breeze ruffling my hair. I felt lighter, leaving Sicily behind. The poverty, the war, Adrian: I let the sea air blow it all away, like smoke. If only I were returning to Gray and England, instead of heading off on some ill-considered pilgrimage with an overwrought actress.

"Luca mustn't know. Ever." Francesca grabbed both of my hands and clasped them to her breast. "Swear to me now, *carissima*. You'll never tell a soul. Not a soul, do you hear?"

I remembered how patiently Luca had spoken to her on the set. No wonder he was short-tempered with the rest of us. Keeping this woman on an even keel was a full-time job—one that now seemed to have fallen to me.

"I won't breathe a word," I said, wiggling my fingers to loosen my hands from her grip. "But can you tell me why we're doing this now? Couldn't it wait until after the film festival?"

"*Carissima,* you do not understand. After the film festival, Luca will go back to his wife. This is my only chance."

"Your only chance at what?"

"To conceive his child."

She had to be kidding. Whoever he was, this so-called saint of hers, surely he wouldn't take kindly to the request of a mistress who wanted to have a baby in order to pressure her married lover into leaving his wife. One minute in the confession booth and Francesca would be cast out in scorn, forced to do penance on her knees, renounce Luca and pledge herself to a life of virtue. I didn't know much about Catholicism, but I'd seen *The Song of Bernadette.* If the virgin maiden played by Jennifer Jones was barely worthy of salvation, what would Padre Pio make of a fallen woman like Francesca? I dreaded the moment when the good father gave her a piece of his mind. More urgently, however, I dreaded getting back in the car with her. Given the way she drove, our chances of reaching the remote monastery on the Adriatic coast in one piece were slim.

"Francesca, do you know how to get there?"

The actress shrugged. "We can ask people. I'm telling you, Padre Pio is famous."

"We're about to dock. Let's buy a map, just to be on the safe side," I said. "Then you can navigate and I'll drive. How does that sound?"

"Ah, you want to drive the spider. Well, why not?" Francesca pinched my cheek indulgently. "We're having an adventure, *carissima.* I've never been to this part of Italy, you know. Nobody comes here. It's quite barbaric."

★ ★ ★ ★ ★

Castellaneta, a small town in Italy's instep, had only one thing going for it, but it was a pretty big thing as far as Francesca and I were concerned. Rudolph Valentino was born there.

"Those eyes of his," gushed my companion. "A woman could lose herself in them."

"Soulful," I agreed. "And the way he kissed!"

"Divino!"

"Divino!" I echoed. We looked at one another and laughed out loud. In the port of Reggio di Calabria, Francesca had bought a road map of southern Italy and an illustrated guidebook to the region. Before we'd gotten very far along the highway that wound north along the Mediterranean, she'd already planned our itinerary. If we timed it right, we'd reach Castellaneta in time for lunch and could still be in San Giovanni Rotondo for the evening Benediction.

I drove with the top down, wearing a new pair of sunglasses I'd bought myself in the port city. My head was full of Valentino, scenes from his movies alternating with old newsreel footage of his funeral. It was all before I was born—he died in 1926—but Father had an extensive library of silent films and once I discovered the great Latin Lover, I watched everything I could find, even his villain pictures.

Leaving the coastal highway, we turned inland, up steep mountain roads and down into valleys where goats grazed amid a tinkling of bells. The hillsides were lush with wild orchids and golden gorse, the air fresh with the scent of rosemary, triggering memories of California. Perhaps it was time to go back to America instead of returning to England, I was thinking. Gray was at home in the London theater world, but I'd have better luck finding work in Hollywood and besides, I'd grown tired of being an expatriate. Four years was a long time to have been away.

Francesca's guidebook sent us to the Bar Valentino and it was there we dined, surrounded by still images of the actor from his best-known films.

"Do you remember how he danced the tango?" I reminisced, drawing her attention to a photo of Valentino in gaucho attire from *The Four Horsemen of the Apocalypse.*

"*Carissima,* I have lived that scene so often in my head, I feel as if I were the Argentinean *signorina* he takes in his arms." She pointed to a picture of *The Sheik* that showed Valentino on the verge of kissing a reluctant Agnes Ayres.

"I am not accustomed to having my orders disobeyed," she said. Valentino's line.

"And I am not accustomed to obeying orders," I responded in the haughty tone I imagined Ayres's character would have used, had the picture not been a silent.

Francesca sighed and shook her head. "Foolish woman!"

If only I could freeze the frame and leave us in that moment, under the smoldering gaze of a dozen Rudolph Valentinos. The simple food we ate—wild greens cooked with fava beans and drizzled with olive oil—brought us even more fully into the great screen lover's world. Here were his earthy origins, in this sun-baked town perched on a cliff, its narrow streets winding up to a stately church where we decided the legendary actor must have been baptized. For the first time since setting off that morning, I was glad we'd come, glad for the crazy impulse that had brought us to this charming place where the spirit of old Hollywood still reigned. Why not live a little! Enjoy what Italy had to offer, take home a better souvenir than the memory of that day in the duchess's orchard with Adrian or the macabre Palermo catacombs? And speaking of souvenirs, before we left Castellaneta, I'd have to buy a postcard for Father. He'd always regretted that he hadn't had the opportunity to direct Valentino.

Francesca called for the bill and I repaired to the lavatory.

Mere minutes later, I returned to find the actress frantic. She'd dumped the contents of her satchel onto the table and was rooting through her possessions, searching for her purse. A few of the other diners had turned around in their seats to watch the unfolding drama. Across the room, I saw our waiter conferring with a short man in a suit, most likely the proprietor. Francesca followed my gaze.

"Quickly, go look in the car!" she commanded in a stage whisper as the two men headed toward our table. "It might have fallen under one of the seats."

I hurried outside, grateful for the cautious instinct that had made me put the top up and lock the doors although I'd parked directly in front of the restaurant. The Alfa attracted attention everywhere we went, and I hadn't liked the idea of leaving it open and unattended. I'd come to feel rather protective about Luca's car. Not so much as a single scratch had marred its shiny red body when Francesca and I took off at daybreak, and I intended to return it in the same condition. But the wallet was not in the spider—I checked everywhere—and now it was my turn to panic. We'd left the villa in such a flurry that I hadn't thought to bring additional cash. I had plenty of money, but it was all in my room, tucked beneath my stockings in a bureau drawer. I counted out the lire in my wallet with painstaking care, tallying the sums in my head. Italian money came in huge denominations, but when you did the math, you found it was practically worthless. All told, I had the equivalent of thirty-seven dollars.

The trip to Padre Pio would have to wait for another time (a prospect that did not displease me). After I paid for the meal, I doubted whether we'd have enough left over for a full tank of gas. It would be touch-and-go, simply getting back to the ferry port, and most likely we'd have to take an expensive taxi ride from Messina to Taormina. So much for adventures, I thought to myself as I went back inside the Bar Valentino to break the news to Francesca.

"Ah, Cara. Come meet *signore* Bardi."

I'd expected to be accosted the instant I walked in the door. Instead, I was greeted by the sight of the actress and the proprietor sitting cozily at the bar, sharing a bottle of liqueur. *Signore* Bardi rose from his seat and came to usher me over.

"*Piacere, signorina,*" he said, beaming. With a flourish, he bowed and kissed my hand, his dark eyes searching mine, Latin-lover style. Only *signore* Bardi was small and balding, with a squint that he was apparently too vain to correct by wearing glasses, so the effect was less Valentino, more Jack Benny.

"*Piacere,*" I repeated. Francesca caught my eye behind *signore* Bardi's back and winked. Struggling to maintain a straight face, I allowed myself to be seated at the bar and accepted a *digestivo*. Every region of Italy had its own recipe for after-dinner liqueurs, our host explained, and most were closely guarded secrets. This particular amaro was made with herbs and citrus peel, a distillation that had been in his family for close to a century.

I took a sip and must have made a face as the sharpness registered on my tongue. "Oh, it's too bitter!" I exclaimed, putting down my glass, but even before I finished speaking, the taste in my mouth had changed to a vanilla-like sweetness that smoothed out the edges delightfully. "No, I take it back. It's sweet." I raised the glass to my lips and took another sip. "It's wonderful!" I concluded. My companions both laughed.

"Bitter and sweet," said *signore* Bardi. "Here we say it is layered with contradictions, *signorina*. Like life itself."

Francesca eyed him with new appreciation. "Layered with contradictions. *Esattamente!*"

Naturally our host wouldn't hear of us paying for the meal. Francesca's purse had obviously been "lifted" while we were in Reggio de Calabria; *signore* Bardi was ashamed of the thieving ways of his fellow southern Italians. And much as he appreciated our desire to see Padre Pio, he didn't like the thought of two ladies making such a trip unescorted. If we could wait until morning, he offered to accompany us himself. There were rooms upstairs, and his wife would see to it that we were comfortable. Truly, it would be a great honor to have a famous actress as his guest.

Gracious as always, Francesca regretted that we could not avail ourselves of his hospitality. But if *signore* Bardi would lend us some money so that we could complete the pilgrimage to Padre Pio, the actress promised to visit again and repay him in person.

"*Volontieri,*" he said. With pleasure. Extracting a billfold from the inner pocket of his jacket, he offered her everything he had. Francesca took half of what he'd offered, which still looked like a generous amount, and thanked him effusively. She led the way to the Alfa, which she insisted on driving, to make up for lost time. I braced myself for another harrowing trip.

The moment we were out of the town, Francesca pulled off the road. "We're not taking any more chances," she said, stuffing the bills from *signore* Bardi inside her bra and instructing me to do the same with my remaining lire. She'd accepted the loss of her purse philosophically—rather too philosophically, I thought. She now spoke as if our fate were entirely in Padre Pio's hands, as if the good father were drawing us to him the way a magnet attracts metal.

"Do you think he'll accept me?" I wondered aloud, more to distract myself from Francesca's driving than because I needed an answer. I wasn't raised a Catholic, wasn't raised in any religion, unless you counted Father's bohemianism. More to the point, I'd lost my virginity at seventeen, given birth to a child out of wedlock and, until recently, had carried on a passionate affair with a man I had no hope of marrying. I felt no shame about any of this. Regrets, yes, but only because I kept falling in love with the wrong men. Wouldn't Padre Pio regard me as a sinner?

Francesca took my concerns seriously. Some years ago, she told me, a man had confessed to Padre Pio that he didn't believe in God. Padre Pio had blessed him all the same. "Don't worry," the good father was said to have responded. "God believes in you." The man became one of his greatest disciples from that moment forward.

"*Carissima*, Padre Pio has a plan for us. I told you already, he summoned me in a dream."

In the face of such certainty, I couldn't resist playing devil's advocate. "What if his plan for you was to become his disciple? Would you give everything up?"

"Everything," Francesca said.

"Including Luca?"

"He'd never ask me to do that. Luca needs me. I am his muse."

Who was I to argue? Not when Francesca was driving at breakneck speed down twisty mountain roads, passing slower vehicles on the uphill stretches, coming perilously close to the edge of the narrow highway. There were no guardrails here, but planted along some of the more treacherous curves were impromptu shrines: a simple cross stuck in the ground, surrounded by flowers and religious objects. I kept silent, but something in my posture must have conveyed skepticism, because Francesca returned to the subject.

"You think I should give him up, don't you?" Even around the sound of the wind in my ears and the grinding of gears as we were brought up short behind a little turquoise pick-up filled with burlap sacks, I could hear the edge in her voice. The last thing in the world I wanted was to antagonize her. Already I anticipated a scene when Francesca learned, as I was sure she would, that the good father was not her ally. If she saw me as being on his side, I feared that I'd bear the brunt of her indignation, and I'd seen enough of her moods to know that the trip back would be hellish enough without setting myself up as her adversary.

"Avanti, avanti!" Francesca shouted at the driver of the pick-up, who was keeping to the center of the road in an effort to prevent his load from shifting, chugging more and more slowly up the hill. Whatever was in those burlap bags must have been quite heavy; the little truck was barely moving. Meanwhile, Francesca was growing more frustrated by the minute. Judiciously, I tried to distract her with a bit of gossip about Valentino. Pola Negri, the silent film star he'd been involved with at the time of his death, was an occasional guest at the lodge. She and Father had worked together at Paramount, and Gray told me they'd had an affair, probably the straw that broke the camel's back as far as his mother was concerned because, given Negri's fame, their liaison was quite public. Negri claimed that Valentino had doubts about his manliness: this from a man, I told Francesca, quoting Negri, who made love like a tiger!

"All men have doubts about their manliness," she said, unimpressed. We were approaching the crest of the hill and Francesca's frustration had reached its limit. Leaning on the horn, she pressed the accelerator to the floor and finally succeeded in getting around the little pick-up. I caught the eye of the driver and gave him an apologetic smile as we zoomed past. He looked a bit like Valentino, dark hair, hooded eyes, and a sensuous mouth—were all the men in this part of Italy so handsome?

Approaching the city of Bari, a major junction on our route, we got our first glimpse of the Adriatic. The landscape changed dramatically, the browns and greens of the mountainous terrain we'd been traveling through giving way to startling white limestone cliffs that rose straight up out of the sea. Here the buildings were so white, and the late afternoon sun so strong, that even wearing my new sunglasses, it hurt to look at them.

We stopped at a gas station where we both freshened up while the attendant filled the tank and checked the oil. A small crowd of auto enthusiasts, all men, had gathered around the Alfa to admire its engine while the hood was up, and our return occasioned some risqué comments, but as with the laborers at the duchess's wedding banquet, Francesca proved herself equal to the challenge. Our new friends informed her that the trip to San Giovanni Rotondo would take a little under three hours, although there was some dispute over the best route. The fastest way to go would be to take the highway connecting Bari with Foggia, the closest large city to Padre Pio's monastery, but portions of the road remained to be finished and traffic moved slowly in the areas still under construction. The coastal road to Manfredonia was only two lanes, but we'd have a clear run and beautiful views.

"What do you think, *carissima*?" Francesca asked, her spirits restored by so much male attention. I opted for the coastal route, which had the virtue of being flatter, with fewer twists and turns, but regretted my decision almost instantly. Unhindered by curves, and anxious about the time, Francesca drove like she was trying out for the Grand Prix. This was bad for my nerves, but it was worse for the car.

"Francesca, is that smoke?"

"Smoke? What are you talking about?"

"I think there's smoke coming out of the engine."

"Nonsense. I don't see any smoke."

We were just south of Trani when the Alfa broke down, smoke billowing from beneath the hood in such quantities that we could hardly see where we were going. Francesca pulled over and collapsed into tears.

I didn't know much about cars, but I thought the Alfa could probably be repaired. The tricky part would be paying for it. The more expensive the car, the more you spent to get it fixed; I'd heard Father complain often enough about the cost of maintaining his various automobiles. Did Francesca have enough bills in her bra to cover a tow truck, on top of the repairs? I was still mulling the problem over in my mind, while trying to calm Francesca down, when a familiar turquoise pick-up braked alongside us.

"Oh, Dio. What does *he* want?" Francesca muttered under her breath.

No question about it, the driver was the spitting image of Valentino. "Ladies, do you need assistance?"

"Thank you . . ." I started to say, but Francesca cut me off.

"We're fine," she said, turning her back to him and making a show of looking for something in her satchel.

Valentino cast his eyes toward the hood of the car, which was still smoking. I was also aware of a burning smell. With a shrug, he pulled away and continued along his route.

"Why were you so rude?" I demanded. "Someone offers to help us and you turn him away!"

Francesca had found her compact and was powdering her nose. "*Carissima,* you're too trusting."

"I'm just being practical. We ought to try and get Luca's car fixed, not just abandon it by the side of the road."

"He's a foreigner," she said, snapping the compact shut.

I wasn't fluent enough to pick up on accents—certainly not from one sentence—but I didn't see what difference it made, whether Valentino was Italian or not. In the ten minutes or so we'd been sitting by the side of the road, he was the only motorist who'd even slowed down to see what was wrong. We didn't have to go with him in the pick-up, but at the very least, we might have asked him to send help when he reached the next town.

In fact, that's exactly what he'd done, although I didn't learn this until later. I'd gotten out of the car and was attempting to pry open the hood when a tow truck arrived from the opposite direction. The driver made a U-turn when he saw us and backed his truck in front of the Alfa. Francesca rushed over to speak with him and before we knew it, we were all three of us crowded into the front seat on the way to his garage, the Alfa in tow.

"You see, *carissima*. It is as I said," she whispered in English. "Padre Pio is watching over us." I made a noncommittal sound, which she took for assent. Truly, I had no faith that we would make it to the monastery, or anywhere else for that matter, on our limited funds. Our mechanic friend, Guido, seemed delighted at the opportunity to work on such a fine machine, but he probably thought we were two rich women from Rome who would be willing to pay through the nose for his services. What choice did we have?

My skepticism turned to outright disbelief when we arrived at Guido's garage, a small building on a side street near the docks and very much a one-man operation. Fortunately for us, it was a slow day. Either that, or Guido didn't get many customers. Francesca had already explained the reason for our trip, and the need for haste if we were to make it to San Giovanni Rotondo in time for evening prayers. Now, as Guido got the car down and prepared to start working on the engine, she began pacing the shop.

"How long will it take?"

Guido looked up from the engine and wiped his brow with an oil-smeared hand. "*Signora*, I need to find out what is wrong with the car. Then I will know if I can fix it."

"How long?" she persisted, consulting her watch and frowning with impatience.

"Go take a walk," he said, giving her a little nudge toward the door. "See the sites. Come back in two hours."

"Two hours! We don't have that much time!" With a flourish, she pulled the remaining lire out of her bra and handed them all to him. "I'll give you everything I have if you can get the car running in half an hour," she said.

"Francesca!"

To his credit, Guido refused to take the money. "There are morning prayers, are there not, *signora*?"

We had no choice but to leave Guido to his repairs. The only site worth visiting, according to Francesca's guidebook, was the cathedral of San Nicola il Pellegrino. Diligently, we set off through the narrow streets of the old medieval quarter, stopping for a glass of lemonade in a quiet café along the way.

The cathedral turned out to be an imposing structure with huge bronze doors set on a plaza overlooking the harbor. Inside the nave was a statue of the Madonna and it was there, as she paused to light a candle to the virgin, that Francesca herself received the tribute of several fans, local women who recognized her despite the widow's disguise. She looked like one of them, which seemed to endear her even more to the devout group.

"*Signora* Vitelli! Is it really her? Shhh, can't you see she's praying?"

The whispers were impossible to ignore. Francesca rose from her knees and nodded at the women, indicating that they should follow her outside. She was prepared to sign autographs, but it was they who wanted to give her something, some token by which she might remember them when she returned to her glamorous life in Rome. My opinion of the actress went up a notch or two as I watched how she treated her admirers. She was grateful for their homage, but unlike the Hollywood stars I knew, she conveyed her appreciation in a way that did not take their reverence for granted. Rather, she seemed touched, humbled even. With downcast eyes, she told them that we had just stopped in Trani on our way to attend a Mass with Padre Pio.

"Ah, Padre Pio." With something approaching awe, the women expressed their approval of our mission. Were we going to confess our sins to the sainted father?

"I'm going to lay my problem at his feet!" proclaimed Francesca. At this, one of the group stepped forward and pressed a rosary into her hand. Fighting back tears, the actress brought the beads to her lips, then clutched them to her heart. *"Grazie.* Bless you, *signora."* If she was acting, she gave the performance of a lifetime.

Guido had the engine running, but he warned us that the Alfa might very well fail again; one of the hoses was cracked, and he'd had to improvise a replacement. Indeed, the smell of burning oil permeated the small garage. Francesca was all for resuming our journey immediately, regardless of the risk, but the mechanic refused to surrender the car until he was satisfied that it wouldn't break down again.

"Come," he said. "You can wait here while I go to find a better hose." He showed us to a room at the back of his shop in which he'd set up a table and two chairs, a cot, and a hot plate. A sink stood in the corner: Spartan accommodations, but everything looked clean and the floor had been recently swept. A few hooks on the wall held items of male clothing, and there was a shaving kit on a shelf by the sink, a razor and a stubby brush laid out neatly on a towel, awaiting use. Perhaps Guido spent the occasional night in his garage when the work got heavy.

I washed my face and hands in the basin, lay down on the cot, and closed my eyes. We'd set off on our journey so early, and my cramps had not subsided. More than this, the ups and

downs of traveling with Francesca had worn me out. I couldn't
wait to return to Taormina and leave the entire drama behind,
but the ordeal wasn't even half over. Sleep, a spell of oblivion,
seemed like the only way to brace myself for what lay ahead.

"Yes, that's right, *carissima*. Rest." Francesca herself was too
keyed up to sit down. Back and forth, back and forth. I thought
the sound of her ceaseless pacing would keep me awake, but the
clicking of her heels on the cement floor grew rhythmic,
comforting, like white noise.

Some hours later, I opened my eyes to an empty room. It was
pitch black inside the garage, but when I looked out the shop's
single window, I could see the sky lightening over the sea. The
Alfa was still sitting in the middle of the garage with its hood
up, but Guido's tow truck was gone. Francesca must have
bribed the mechanic to take her to San Giovanni Rotondo for
morning Mass, or perhaps she'd charmed him as she'd charmed
signore Bardi and the women in the church.

I don't know why, but I wasn't worried. To tell the truth, it
was a relief to be free of Francesca, free for a time of the nervous
energy that kept me on edge, trying to anticipate her next mood.
The smallest thing might set her off, and who could guess what
that might be? I drew a deep breath and let it out slowly, breath-
ing fully for the first time in days. She'd be back, and Guido
would finish repairing the car eventually. One thing I could do
while I waited was to phone the villa and let Luca know where
we were, but I'd have to place the call from a post office, and it
was only just coming up to five in the morning.

To kill time, I decided to have breakfast. I'd had nothing but
a lemonade since our lunch in Castellaneta the day before. I
cleaned myself as best I could in Guido's sink, combed my hair
and put on a little lipstick before venturing outside in search of
a café. All the places in the vicinity of the garage were tightly
shuttered, but I heard activity down by the docks. Fishermen

setting off for the day, no doubt, but from somewhere I caught a strain of accordion music, and the sound of children's laughter. Wrapping my shawl around my head and shoulders, I crossed the road and peered over the stone sea wall to get a better look at the beach below.

Gypsies, a gathering of some twenty people, were camped at the base of the wall. There, sheltered from the wind and out of view from casual passersby, the men lounged about, playing instruments and smoking as the woman cooked over an open fire. I saw girls, some quite little, helping their mothers. Farther along the beach, boys raced along the hard sand at the water's edge, daring one another to dart ever closer to the waves. The trick was to avoid getting wet, but the urge to show off in front of one's fellows proved too strong. I watched as one boy after another tempted fate, only to get drenched by an unexpected wave.

I'd seen Gypsies in Sicily. Luca had filmed a group we'd come across one evening, our original destination forgotten in his excitement at having discovered the picturesque scene. While he sought permission to shoot them, Salvatore was already at work setting up lights and directing the crew around. A handful of children approached, aiming for a closer look at the equipment, but the gaffer shooed them away. I'd detected no menace in the children's curiosity and had said as much to Adrian, who'd sided with Salvatore.

"Little thieves, all of them," he'd said. Lazy, dirty, and dishonest, they caused trouble everywhere they went.

The Gypsies on the beach in Trani were intent on their own activities, and the women and girls struck me as quite industrious. In the scant early morning light, and covered in black from head to toe, I was able to observe them unobtrusively. From where I stood, elbows propped on the stone ledge, the smell of their cooking wafted up toward me, roasted meat seasoned with pungent herbs. My stomach grumbled.

"Hungry, *signorina*?" Valentino was standing beside me, a smile playing upon his lips. How long had he been observing me as I watched the Gypsies, thinking myself unseen? I found myself blushing, and wished I were wearing an outfit more flattering than widow's weeds.

"Starving!" I used a delightful Italian expression I'd learned in school that translated as "hungry as a wolf."

My companion laughed. "Wolves can be dangerous when they're hungry," he said. "Should I be afraid?"

"I am very hungry," I admitted. "But I'll spare your life if you can point me to a decent café. Or even a lousy café. So long as the coffee's hot, I won't complain."

He took my hand and led me down to the beach. "Would you care to join us?"

CHAPTER NINE:
FATA MORGANA

We descended a stone staircase to the beach and wove our way around the tents and caravans planted helter-skelter on the sand. I kept my head covered—the Gypsy women were all wearing scarves, I noticed—but I was still an outsider, *gadji* in their language. Valentino was no less an outsider, but he'd lived among Gypsies and knew their ways.

Protocol demanded that I be presented to the head of the Gypsy family before taking my place with the women. This was not a straightforward operation; a female did not simply walk up to a male and shake his hand, particularly when that male was seated on the ground. Also, when meeting him, she had to be careful not to stand too close, lest her skirt brush against his body and defile him. All of this Valentino hastily explained as he led me over to the gathering.

"You're not Italian," he said. "Are you English?" Francesca was right; the more I heard him speak, the more certain I became that he was not Italian. For one thing, he spoke more slowly than any Italian I'd ever encountered, and the melody of his words sounded different.

"American."

"American! I know many Americans," he said, switching to English, but still with that lilting melody. "All of them soldiers. There was a camp here, did you know?"

"A camp? An army base, do you mean?"

"A camp. For displaced persons." A sadness came into his

eyes as he said this, an expression of such deep sorrow that I was moved to touch his face. Just for an instant.

"Najdroższa," he said softly. A Polish word his mother used to say. I didn't know it at the time, of course, but I sensed that it meant something sweet.

The Gypsy leader was a small man, gaily dressed in striped trousers and wearing a bright blue vest over his bare torso, gold medallions around his neck, and rings on every finger. When he smiled, I saw that he had several gold teeth as well. I stood obediently by Valentino's side while he made the introductions, pretending not to notice the attention I was attracting from the other men in the group. I couldn't understand a word of the conversation going on around us, but its ribald tone was clear enough. As with the camera crew in Sicily, gestures spoke more eloquently than words and needed no translation.

"They think you're my woman," Valentino whispered. He seemed to find the situation humorous and I couldn't help but share his amusement. The whole thing was surreal: me stranded in some remote town in southern Italy, being introduced into a tribe of Gypsies, my fate in the hands of a handsome stranger whose real name I didn't know. And I didn't even care! Luca would be jealous when he heard about my adventure, assuming Francesca returned to fetch me and we made it back to the villa in one piece.

Valentino next brought me over to meet the women. As with the men, there was a hierarchy within the group, authority vested in a pair of grandmothers who sat near the campfire, supervising the work of the others. Neither looked out of her forties. Gypsies married in their teens; by the time a girl was my age, she'd have given birth to several children, but life was hard for Gypsy women and few made it into old age.

All of this I learned from Valentino after he and I were

banished to the margins of the gathering. Everything had seemed to be going so well. Valentino was clearly a favorite with the two older women, who paid me no notice whatsoever but bantered with him for a good five minutes. Then one grandmother gave me a wary look and muttered something to the other grandmother, who turned her full scrutiny to my lower body. Had the rumbling of my stomach offended them? Valentino was acting uncomfortable all of a sudden. The grandmothers were sniffing the air, quizzing him intently. The word *gadji* was used repeatedly, and not in a friendly way.

"They want to know if it is your time of month."

For goodness sake, how could they tell? Too embarrassed to meet his eyes, I nodded and looked at the ground. Next thing I knew, we were off by ourselves, eating stew from plates that would be thrown away after we'd used them, drinking acid coffee out of tin cups also intended for the trash, all owing to my impurity. Valentino had spread his jacket on the sand and we were sitting quite close. Every so often, his fingertips would graze my arm as he reached up to brush his black hair away from his face, his touch like warm rain on my skin. I felt as if I'd known him forever.

"Cigarette?" He pulled a blue and white cardboard box from his shirt pocket.

I accepted a Gitane and a light. "Thank you." Inhaling, I felt the burn at the back of my throat as I drew the smoke into my lungs. Some of Gray's blacklisted Hollywood friends smoked Gitanes. Like everything French in those days, they were quite fashionable, but were much stronger than my usual brand, Lucky Strikes, and it was all I could do not to choke on the first few puffs.

I've given up smoking now, but every so often, when we're performing together in some jazz club on the French Riviera, I'll be brought back to that morning on the beach in Trani.

Wreathed in a haze of the sharp-smelling tobacco, the sight of the Gypsies grouped by the fire, the boys dashing in and out of the sea. The aliveness that suffused my entire being as we sat and smoked, Valentino and I, in companionable silence. And the music, the sound of those rousing, haunting tunes when he was eventually persuaded to pick up his violin and join the other musicians.

Gypsy jazz. How to describe the way I felt the first time I heard them play? Two guitars doing the work of a rhythm section, an accordionist keying harmonies in the background, and Valentino's violin carrying the melody. The cadence was swing, but with a melancholy air. Jaunty tunes that shaded imperceptibly into a minor key. You wanted to tap your toes, dance to the exuberant beat, but the more you listened, the more you realized that the exuberance was just on the surface. Layered beneath was a pool of sadness, and that's what lingered even as the last note faded away.

The sadness was all in the violin. Valentino's fingers moved gracefully along the fingerboard as his bow danced across the strings, inviting you to explore the dark recesses of his soul. I don't know how he managed to convey his entire history in his playing, but later, when he told me the actual details of his life, it was as if I already knew everything that mattered.

"*Carissima!* Thank God!" Francesca materialized out of nowhere and embraced me with tears in her eyes, the rosary clutched in her fist. I was still off to the side of the Gypsy gathering, absorbed in the music, and hadn't seen her until she was directly in front of me, but over her shoulder I could track the course she'd taken through the assembly. Like a tornado, she'd left damage in her wake: the men were all standing, shaking their heads and looking after her in disbelief, the women had formed an angry little knot around the two grandmothers, who were sending decidedly evil looks our way.

Abruptly, the music stopped. Valentino conferred with someone—Guido (I hadn't recognized the mechanic at first without his blue coveralls)—while the other musicians looked on. A minute or two elapsed as I patted Francesca's back, straining to overhear the two men's conversation over the sound of her sobbing.

"Shhh, shhh," I murmured. "It's okay." But Francesca was too distraught to quiet down. She repeated the words "no hope" several times, along with appeals to Mary Magdalene, the patron saint of fallen women.

"Oh, help me, Maria. I swear I will die! I am not strong enough to give him up." With this, the actress slipped from my arms and knelt in the sand to pray.

While Francesca was on her knees, voicing her laments, a delegation of Gypsy women had begun to make their way toward us, headed by the two grandmothers. As they approached, faces set in fury, I was relieved to see that Valentino and Guido had broken off their conversation and were also moving in our direction. Unfortunately, the women had a head start and they reached us first.

"*Gadji!*" The grandmothers grabbed Francesca, each taking an arm and yanking her to her feet. The others moved to form a circle around the three of them, blocking me out. A chorus of invective in the Romani language ensued, each woman vying to express her outrage through both words and body language. Francesca was too stunned to react, and my efforts to shoulder my way into the circle to defend her were repulsed. I looked imploringly at our rescuers, willing them to intervene before she was harmed.

Then, as if by magic, the shouting ceased. The circle parted of its own accord and Valentino was admitted into the center. Interposing himself between Francesca and the angry grandmothers, he began speaking to the group of women in a soft, persuasive voice.

Guido arrived at my side. "*Signorina,* please forgive me," he said. "I wasn't happy, leaving you in the middle of the night, but the *signora* was determined to go to the Mass, and I thought it best to accompany her." He inclined his head toward Valentino. "I asked Jakub to keep an eye on you until we got back."

So, it hadn't been pure chance, our encounter. "Thank you. He took good care of me. What did you say his name was?"

"Jakub." He pronounced it *ya-cob,* a name I'd never heard before.

"Ya-cob," I repeated, struggling to form the unfamiliar syllables. Valentino was better, by far. "What happened in San Giovanni Rotondo? Did Padre Pio turn her away?"

The mechanic shrugged. He had not been there in the church. All he had to go on was Francesca's distress. She'd cried the entire way back and, from what he'd pieced together, it appeared that the good father had refused to hear her confession.

Now it looked as if she was being given the chance to confess after all. Valentino was asking her questions in front of the other women, and translating her responses into Romani. Initially his questions elicited only a word or two in response, but Francesca's listeners were soon caught up in the story and began posing follow-up questions of their own, which Valentino translated into Italian. The tone of the interchange shifted; the Gypsy women were obviously moved by the actress's plight. A lengthy account of Luca's insensitivity, culminating in a blow-by-blow description of the catacombs visit and the argument that had taken place in the car just two nights before, all faithfully conveyed by Valentino, succeeded in winning them over entirely. Whatever indignation her behavior had provoked was now redirected toward Luca.

One of the grandmothers turned to Valentino and issued him instructions. Pointing to his violin and bow, which he was still holding, she sent him back to the company of musicians. I watched him confer with the accordionist and the two guitarists. Moments later, the four struck up a lively tarantella.

"We dance now," said the grandmother, taking Francesca's hand and leading her closer to the musicians. The Gypsy men drew back as the women approached, creating a clear space for them to occupy. Some clapped as the women launched into their dance, others whistled or shouted as the dance grew more frenzied, the song's tempo speeding up in time with the women's exertions. I found it nearly impossible to distinguish among the various elements of the spectacle. The activity seemed fused with the music, the smoke from the campfire, the swirling skirts in their bright patterns. All combined in a wild explosion of movement and sound, a feverish hallucination that enveloped performers and onlookers alike.

Guido and I were the only people not caught up in the madness. To be honest, it frightened me, the abandon with which the women threw themselves into the tarantella, Francesca especially. She seemed possessed, eyes wide but unseeing, limbs twitching, bare feet stamping the sand as she flung her body about, hoarse cries, animal-like in their intensity, escaping from her open mouth. Surely she could not keep it up, this frenetic motion. She looked to me like she was struggling, the way a swimmer flails her arms before being engulfed. I voiced my concern to Guido.

"*Affogata*," he agreed. Drowned.

Drowned. The word brought back the memory of Vivien face-down in the pool. Again, I considered the possibility that my mother had been carrying on an affair, but now a darker scenario suggested itself. What if she too had been rejected?

Might she not have killed herself? It didn't make sense, had never made sense (although as a child I'd accepted it as one of those aspects of the adult world I'd understand someday) that Vivien had ended up in the pool by accident, and wearing her nightgown, no less. Unlike Geoffrey, she was not in the habit of going for an early morning swim. Thinking back, I couldn't remember her taking more than a cursory dip, and she never went in the water without wearing a bathing cap to protect her hairdo. My mother was always well coiffed, her auburn hair set in smooth waves for day, or pinned up into an elegant chignon in the evening when she and Father were going out.

A flood of grief washed over me, all those long-ago feelings of abandonment converging into one powerful impulse. I had to resolve the mystery of Vivien's death. For too long I'd accepted the version of events I'd been given, but deep within I'd sensed there was more to the story. Now I knew where to look for answers and, while I didn't relish dredging up the sordid details of an affair, I intended to follow my hunch and uncover the truth, learn who my mother really was and why her life had ended so tragically.

Francesca eventually stopped dancing. The Gypsy women took turns hugging and kissing her goodbye. *"Grazie, grazie,"* she said, smiling through tears of gratitude. Supported by Guido on one side and Valentino on the other, she allowed herself to be escorted back to the Alfa, which was parked on the street in front of the garage. Her feelings toward the handsome violinist had undergone a complete reversal. She was now quite smitten.

"Jakub," she said as he handed her into the car. "Even his name is a song. Do all Gypsies have such lyrical names, or only the musical ones?"

Valentino smiled. "I'm not a Gypsy, *signora.*"

"Not a Gypsy?" She turned to Guido for support. "Impossible! Only a Gypsy could play an instrument so seductively!"

"He is Polish," the mechanic said.

"Ah, Polish!" The actress gave a dismissive little wave of her hand. "It amounts to the same thing. A romantic people, the Poles."

I excused myself and went into the garage to use the lavatory, where I spent a fair amount of time staring into the dusty mirror over the sink, brooding. The real Rudolph Valentino made light of his romantic allure. "I am merely the canvas upon which women paint their dreams," he once said. Jakub had a similar self-deprecating air. In contrast to the actors I'd fallen for in the past, he displayed not the slightest trace of ego, and yet he possessed a personal magnetism that made him impossible to ignore—or to forget. Knowing that he'd merely been babysitting me on orders from Guido made me unbearably sad. His warmth, the affinity I'd sensed between us, was it nothing more than duty on his part, combined with wishful thinking on mine? Or did he sense it too, the feeling that we were one another's true company? I told myself such speculations were pointless. I'd never see him again.

"Thank you for taking care of me," I said as we shook hands and said goodbye.

"It was my pleasure." He bent to kiss my hand. "*Najdroższ*," he murmured on a breath so soft that only I could hear it. The word means dearest. I looked it up.

The return trip was mercifully anti-climatic. Francesca was exhausted, physically and emotionally, and slept for a good deal of the drive. I tried to figure her out as I navigated the winding roads back to the port city. The deep unhappiness she'd displayed before she started dancing seemed to have vanished as suddenly as it had appeared. Was this an indication that it was never real, merely a role the actress put on or discarded at will? Or evidence that there was nothing solid, nothing to Francesca but a succession of appearances, each as plausible as the next?

I was still thinking about it as we neared the coast. Here the wartime damage was more extensive, restoration of the bombed-out towns and ravaged landscape having barely begun. As in Sicily, the wreckage was terrible, but speeding past in the Alfa, it was easy to ignore. Too easy: a mere day had elapsed since I'd set off on this mad adventure of Francesca's, but something had changed inside me. Perhaps it was the actress's self-absorption, her inability to get outside herself, but I was suddenly conscious of my own smallness, the pettiness of my problems in the face of the desolation we'd seen. Entire countries had been laid to waste by the war and ten years later, people were still suffering. Or perhaps they'd always suffered and I'd never noticed.

Descending the mountains into Reggio di Calabria, I caught my first glimpse of Sicily across the Strait of Messina, and there I was presented with a striking mirage. A ghostly castle, its rocky walls crowned by majestic towers, hung in the clouds above the sea. It was the Fata Morgana, an effect of air and light—quite a famous optical illusion, although I'd never heard of it. I braked by the side of the road to get a better view.

"What is it? Is something wrong?" Francesca opened her eyes with a start and looked about in alarm. Following my gaze, she stared in awe at the apparition for a long moment. The mirage was stunning, its form etched in such detail that you'd swear you were looking at a real castle. "Thank you, Maria. *Grazie*," she murmured. Pulling her satchel onto her lap, she fished out the rosary and began to pray. Tears were streaming down her cheeks, but the actress made no effort to wipe them away, so caught up was she in her devotion.

I got out of the car and walked around a bit to stretch my legs. I'd been driving for five hours straight, stopping only once to fill up the tank. What kept me going was the knowledge that Luca would be meeting our ferry in Messina. Before leaving Trani, Francesca had called him collect from the post office. As soon as he'd accepted the charges, she'd launched into a full apology, which soon turned into reassurances that we were okay, that we were on our way home, that Caterina should prepare her famous risotto because we'd be hungry after our trip. Any anger he'd felt upon discovering that we'd absconded in the wee hours of the morning with the Alfa had evidently given way to fears for our safety. Even if Francesca hadn't succeeded in getting Padre Pio to perform a miracle, it seemed that the relationship with Luca would survive—until the next crisis, at least—and I intended to be in London long before that happened.

Alas, a new crisis greeted me as soon as I'd gotten back behind the wheel.

"*Carissima*," said Francesca, opening her compact and powdering her nose. "Will you be able to find your way to Reggio di Calabria?"

"We're practically there," I replied. "And if we get lost, we can always ask directions."

"That's right." Balancing the compact on her knee, she reached inside her satchel and extracted a tube of lipstick. "But listen, *carissima*. You're going to have to make the rest of the trip by yourself."

"What do you mean?"

Francesca held the lipstick aloft. She seemed to be contemplating something of great importance. "No," she decided, returning the tube to the satchel. Reaching inside her bra, the actress extracted a quantity of bills and handed them to me. "Take this," she said. "I won't be needing it."

"Francesca!" I tried to give the money back. A million questions crowded into my mind. "What are you talking about?

Where are you going? What about Luca?"

"Don't be afraid. The good father is watching over us both, I am sure of it. He has called me back, don't you understand?" She must have seen the confusion on my face. "The castle, *carissima*," she said.

"The castle?" I repeated stupidly.

"It was a sign." One hand on the door handle, she leaned in and gave me a kiss on each cheek, Italian style. Then she opened the door and got out of the car.

I sat there, holding a fistful of *signore* Bardi's lire, and watched her walk up the road in the direction we'd come. She'd wrapped the shawl around herself and from the back she looked like any Italian widow. I started the engine and put the car in gear, drove slowly until I was right alongside her.

"Be sensible," I called out over the thrumming of the motor. "You can't walk all the way back to Padre Pio." Francesca tossed her head and kept moving. I didn't know what to do. Short of knocking her unconscious and dragging her back into the passenger seat, how was I going to get her on the ferry?

A horn beeped. Glancing in the rearview mirror, I saw a line of cars and trucks snaking impatiently along behind me.

"Francesca! Get in the car!" I stopped and reached over to open the passenger door. "Please!"

The actress ignored me, but quickened her pace. Cars were coming down the road from the opposite direction, making it impossible for the traffic behind me to pass. More horns beeped. I cursed them under my breath in English and Italian. There was no recourse but to keep driving.

"I'll wait for you up ahead," I shouted. I sped up but was forced to keep going for about a mile before I came to another turn-off where I could park safely. Half a dozen vehicles accelerated past me at speed. I waited until the road was more or less empty and set off down the hill on foot to meet Francesca, mustering arguments in my head.

I can't let you do this. Nothing but a firm, direct appeal would work; Francesca was beyond the reach of reason, I decided. But where was she? I'd walked as far as the place where we'd caught sight of the Fata Morgana and hadn't seen her. Could she have stopped to rest somewhere along the way? I peered along the steep slope, removing my sunglasses for a better view, but could find no sign of her. Retracing my steps to the car, I vowed to wait until she emerged, but the midday sun was hot and even with the top up, sitting in the Alfa had become unbearable.

Had she thrown herself off a cliff? Truly, Francesca was capable of anything. I ran back down the road, pausing here and there to call her name and scanning the landscape down below. I could see no signs of her, no evidence of a tumble down the rocky slope. She seemed to have vanished into thin air. My only comfort was the hope that Francesca had accepted a ride from one of the drivers who'd zoomed by after I pulled off the road. For all I knew, someone had recognized her and she was now being chauffeured to San Giovanni Rotondo by an admiring fan. Conceding defeat, I made my way back to the port alone.

Luca's smile beneath his cool black sunglasses was the first thing I saw as I drove off the ferry. I'd kept the top up on the convertible, so it wasn't until I'd pulled up beside him on the quay that he realized Francesca was not in the car.

"Ciao, bella!" he said, leaning in through the window to kiss me on both cheeks as she had done, less than an hour before.

"Luca, I'm so sorry. I've got to tell you about Francesca. She's not with me."

"I can see that," he said, unruffled.

I opened the door and got out to stand beside him as he turned to scan the passengers coming off the gang plank, shielding his eyes against the glare. "I mean, she's not on the ferry."

"Not on the ferry?" He looked around, as if expecting Francesca to pop out from behind one of the sheds on the dock. "I give up," he said, as if we'd been playing a guessing game. "Where is she?"

"I don't know," I admitted in a quavering voice. All the fatigue and anxiety of the past twenty-four hours caught up with me and I burst into tears. Luca drew me into a fatherly hug, patting my back until I'd calmed down enough to give him an account of what had happened since Francesca and I left the villa. I told him about *signore* Bardi and Guido and the Gypsies on the beach, although I kept Valentino to myself. When I got to the part about the Fata Morgana and Francesca's impromptu decision to return to Padre Pio, how I'd failed to dissuade her from the plan and how I'd then lost sight of her on the road, I was overcome by another wave of sobbing.

Luca grabbed me firmly by the shoulders. "How long ago was this, would you say?"

"A couple of hours. No more."

"You're sure, Cara?" I nodded. "Then it's not too late," he said with relief. I realized that he intended to track her down and begged him to bring me along—I could show him the place where she'd disappeared—but Luca sent me back to the villa with the driver. Francesca might have a change of heart and if she returned, I was to do everything in my power to prevent her from leaving. "Sit on her, if you have to, but keep her with you, do you understand?" I'd never seen him so distraught.

Luca returned alone the following day. He'd managed to find Francesca in San Giovanni Rotondo, but the actress refused to come home. She intended to dedicate her life to the poor, hoping in this way to atone for her promiscuity.

"She told you this?" I asked. He was lying on the couch in the darkened living room with a damp cloth on his forehead.

I'd brought him a couple of aspirin and was trying to get him to swallow them with a glass of water.

Luca sighed theatrically. "She told me to go back to my wife and beg her forgiveness."

Chapter Ten:
Vivien

"Promise me you won't be upset, Cara," said Gray, placing a small packet of correspondence secured with string on the table between us. Half a dozen letters addressed to him at some military training camp in New Jersey. I recognized Vivien's handwriting on the creased envelopes. The careless penmanship, *i*'s dotted on the fly, *t*'s crossed any old place or not at all. She used to write to me when she was away, tourist postcards from the places where she and Father travelled on location. I had a shoebox full of them, which I'd left back at the lodge when we decamped to England. But those were nothing compared to the trove of actual letters in front of me, some of them several pages long, judging from the thickness of the envelopes.

"You've had them all this time? Why didn't you show me sooner?" It hurt to talk; my throat was tight with emotion.

"I wasn't sure you could handle them."

I reached for the packet, but he laid his palm down upon it. "For goodness sake, I'm not a child, Gray."

"Anyone can see that," he agreed, acknowledging my smart Italian attire with an approving nod. But he didn't remove his palm. In fact, I'd just turned twenty-three and we'd gone to Brown's Hotel for afternoon tea to celebrate. It was there, seated in the elegant dining room among well-mannered gentry while sipping perfectly brewed Darjeeling from bone china cups, a tiered silver tray of cut sandwiches, scones, and petit fours on the table between us, that he'd chosen to reveal his secret cache of my mother's letters.

"So why is it that you feel you still need to protect me?" I said, striving with only partial success to hide my exasperation. Was I destined to be forever his baby sister?

My brother took a sandwich from the tray and consumed it in two bites. He picked up the teapot and poured himself another cup, which looked to be mostly dregs. "Ah, I seem to have finished it off," he said. "Would you like me to order another pot?"

I pushed up the sleeves of my cashmere sweater, rested my elbows on the table, and fixed him with a stare. "No, I would not like you to order another pot of tea."

"Scone?" he suggested maddeningly, proffering the tray. "Petit four?"

"Let's cut to the chase," I said. "My mother was having an affair, wasn't she?"

An expression of genuine surprise crossed his face. "An affair?" He appeared to give the matter serious consideration. "No, I don't think she was looking for love. It was approval she was after."

"What do you mean by approval? She was already famous." Absentmindedly, I picked a candied violet off the top of a petit four and crumbled it to pieces between my thumb and forefinger.

"People underestimated your mother. She was so stunning, they didn't care whether she had a brain or not." He paused, as if unsure whether or not to continue.

"Please go on. She was my mother. I deserve to know."

"Poor Vivien," he sighed. "She was so desperate to be taken seriously, not for how she looked, you understand, but for who she was. Or who she wanted to be. She pictured herself as some kind of radical heroine, a modern-day Joan of Arc, charging into battle on behalf of the poor and downtrodden. And that's the tragedy, because she simply wasn't up to the role." He handed me the letters. "It's all in there, you'll see."

Be brave, I told myself. With trembling fingers, I lit a cigarette and smoked it all the way down in an attempt to steady my nerves. Then I untied the string from around the packet, removed the first letter from its envelope, and began to read.

Walden Lodge

August 3, 1942

Darling Gray,

I'd imagine that I'm the last person on earth you expected to hear from. We haven't exactly been close—well, that's putting it mildly! We've barely been on speaking terms since the day we met.

I've been a pill, haven't I? Of course you had every right to resent me. There you were, just back from your first year at Yale, coming to see your father and finding me, a pregnant teenager living at the lodge and about to become your stepmother. "May I call you Vivien?" you asked. What else could you possibly have called me? Not mother, obviously. I'm not even believable as Cara's mother, poor thing. She calls me Vivien, too.

I'm sure you have no idea why I'm writing to you like this, out of the blue. To tell the truth, I have nobody else to confide in. Not Robbie, certainly. You know your father has little interest in politics, except as it relates to making money. I remember when you told him that to his face—at the time I was scandalized—but now I see that you had it right. Hollywood continues the same as always, with its parties and premieres. The show must go on, they say, even as the world burns.

Are you scandalized, darling? If you are, I'll stop. It's just that I feel so alone here. Not only at the lodge, I mean alone in my opinions. You're the only person I can think of who could possibly understand how I feel. Please don't hold it against me, the way I used to be. I'm not the same person you used to know.

As ever,
Vivien

Walden Lodge
August 17, 1942
Darling Gray,

I can't tell you how happy I was to receive your letter. Thank you for writing back so promptly. What's gotten into me, you want to know? I'll tell you in a word. Mexico. I was there with Harry Caldwell, making a musical, of all things. Vincent's idea, and before you say it, yes, I'm being dubbed. The film will be distributed all over Latin America and not only will I be singing, but I'll be speaking Spanish. A saucy señorita with half a dozen suitors, but I ditch them all in the end to run away with Harry. Well, who wouldn't? Such a shame, that he likes the pretty boys. Vincent had his work cut out for him during the shooting, believe you me, keeping Harry's hands off the Mexican crew.

Did you ever meet Diego Rivera when he was in California? Vincent thought that you might have been at the gathering at Charlie Chaplin's. Such passion! He's a very large man. Oh, let's call a spade a spade. He's fat, darling, as big as Oliver Hardy. But women still find him irresistible, and you wouldn't believe how many mistresses he's had. His wife puts up with it. She's a fine artist in her own right and was once quite beautiful. You can see that in her strong features, but she was in dreadful pain when we were there, could barely walk, poor thing. Diego worships her—you should see how tender he was, carrying her to the garden and settling her on cushions so she could paint, coaxing her to eat, feeding her by hand, as if she were a little bird. His body may stray, but his heart and soul will always belong to Frida.

But I want to tell you about his artwork. You must have heard about the murals he's painting all over Mexico? Magnificent scenes of people working, dancing, praying, loving. People of all ages, all races. Diego wants to celebrate the people of Mexico and give them back their history. He wants to change the world.

He reminded me of you, darling. The way you sounded in '36, when you were hot to fight in Spain. "The cause of the Spanish people is our cause," you said. You probably thought I wasn't listening, but I do remember your words, and how Robbie laughed at you. You were so angry! But you were right. Vincent says we had a chance to fight Fascism in Spain and we let it go. This war is the product of our blindness and stupidity. So much death and suffering! It could have been prevented, had we stood up for democracy in Spain . . .

I looked up from my mother's letter. Politics, art, and movie industry gossip all jumbled together. I struggled to sort through the information, picking out the important bits. "What did Vivien mean, about you wanting to fight in Spain?"

"She was referring to the Spanish Civil War." I must have had a blank expression on my face. Gray smiled. "I guess they didn't teach you about it in school. Let's see. How should I explain it?" He pondered the matter for a long moment, time enough for the hotel pianist to launch into the opening stanza of a Noel Coward tune, "Mad About the Boy." A sad smile crossed my brother's face and I imagined he was thinking about Dory. For my part, the lyrics brought Valentino to mind. Months had passed since that morning on the beach with the Gypsies. Why couldn't I forget him? I'd been on a few dates with men I met in London, including an American saxophonist who played in The Crown and Two Chairmen. Margaret had fixed us up, and I liked him well enough, but his music failed to stir my heart.

"All right, imagine this," said Gray. "What if the people of America had elected Adlai Stevenson for president, instead of General Eisenhower?"

"You'd have liked that, wouldn't you?" I remembered how avidly he'd followed the elections in 1952—all of the expatriates did—believing that Stevenson would put an end to the blacklist.

"I'd have liked it, yes. But a lot of people wouldn't have liked it at all. They thought Stevenson was pink. So imagine if General Eisenhower had gotten together the army, and attacked Washington to get rid of Stevenson," he continued. "That's what happened in Spain, you see. They held fair elections and the candidate who won was like Stevenson. Well, not exactly like Stevenson. He was more radical. He wanted to make Spain a true democracy, and make everyone equal. Spain used to be run by the very rich. They had the church on their side, and the army, but the majority of people lived like peasants."

"Peasants?" I interrupted. "It sounds like you're talking about Sicily." I'd told Gray what I'd seen there, about the terrible poverty and how people lived in the streets. It made me sad, remembering the children dressed in rags with their matted hair and dirty faces. The hunger in their eyes.

My brother nodded. "You're getting the picture. Imagine all those peasants finally having a voice! But the general in Spain, Franco, got together an army and attacked the new government in Madrid. The people fought back, but they weren't trained as soldiers. They were just ordinary people, men and women, work-ers, peasants. They didn't even have proper weapons. No tanks, no airplanes. But they had passion! Spain was their country and for the first time, their government was giving them land, and dignity."

"Franco won, didn't he?" I knew that much. There was talk

of Spain around the dining room table at the villa in Taormina, which I'd only half-followed.

"I'm afraid so. But he couldn't have done it alone. He had outside help. Dictators like Hitler and Mussolini started sending troops and bombing Spanish cities from the air. Thousands of innocent Spanish civilians were killed. Women and children, old people, priests and nuns . . ." He stroked his goatee with his thumb and index finger, a stricken look on his face. "It was a bloodbath. There's no other word to describe the horror."

"Wait a minute," I said. "We let this happen? Americans stood by and watched while innocent people got killed? I can't believe that!"

Gray flashed his sad smile again. "There were pictures, Cara. In *Life* magazine! The whole world knew what was going on in Spain."

"Then why didn't we stop it? We could've sent planes too, and tanks, and battleships, like we did in World War II and Korea."

"We were afraid," he said, his tone flat, matter-of-fact. "The new Spanish government—they called themselves the Popular Front, by the way—was made up of a bunch of different parties from liberals in the center all the way to Socialists and Communists on the left. There were even Anarchists who didn't believe in government at all, the kind of people who assassinate leaders and blow things up, just to cause trouble. That scared the leaders of capitalist countries like ours, so when the Germans bombed the hell out of Guernica, we didn't lift a finger to help. A handful of Communists from countries like Britain, France, and Italy sneaked into Spain and joined the Spanish people in their fight. German and Italian Communists went too. They called themselves the International Brigades."

"And that's what you wanted to do, right? Join the International Brigades!" I was seeing a different side of my brother. A younger, more hopeful Gray who still believed in something. Vivien had known this Gray, and it was to him that she was appealing in her letters. She wanted him on her side.

"Ah, yes. I was quite an idealist in those days," he sighed, his bitter self once more. "But in the end I allowed myself to be persuaded not to go. I finished college and left the fighting to others. It wouldn't have made a difference if I had gone," he added. "The whole thing was over by 'thirty-eight and it was clear long before that the Spanish people were doomed. The only country willing to help was the Soviet Union, but their help came with strings attached."

"Strings?"

"They only wanted to help the Communists." A weariness crept into his voice. "Rather than let the Popular Front coalition win, and have the Communists share power with the other parties, they sabotaged their own side. At the time, few of us wanted to believe they were capable of such treachery. Now, of course, it seems entirely plausible."

I'd never asked my brother about his political activities—the ones that had gotten him blacklisted. I assumed he was innocent of whatever he'd been accused of: plotting to overthrow the United States government or spying for the Russians. Now I saw that he was involved up to his eyeballs in "the cause," and guilty in his own mind of betrayal. But it was his own principles he'd betrayed, not his country. And it was these very same principles that had been awakened in my mother. She hadn't found a lover in Mexico. She'd found her purpose.

Walden Lodge
August 30, 1942
Darling Gray,
    Your stories of doing combat maneuvers in the sand at
Atlantic City had us all in stitches. "They're making a soldier

of my boy!" your father said. Don't think he isn't proud of you. I had to laugh, though, when you asked about Hollywood soi-rées. I haven't attended a gala opening in ages, much less hosted one of those "bacchanalian events by the pool," as you call your father's parties. I've lost the taste for it. The world has grown dark and cold, or perhaps it was always that way and I was too vain to notice.

    Tell me, darling, how did you put up with me, all these years? How did you endure my ignorance? Here I've been living a glamorous life, oblivious to the pain and suffering around me, even when it was staring me in the face. Do you remember Maria, the nursemaid we had for Cara? Jobo discovered that she was stealing food from the kitchen and your father fired her, just like that. Of course I felt sorry to see her go. She was a sweet woman, and very good with the baby. I do remember asking why we couldn't give her a second chance. We were in the middle of shooting Napoleon and Josephine *and Cara was still an infant. I had a hard time finding a new person. But Robbie was inflexible on such matters and I was still in awe of him in those days.*

    Do you know what she was stealing? Leftovers. She was taking home table scraps to feed her family. Her husband was sick with tuberculosis, and we didn't pay her very much. Carmelita told me the truth. She still sees Maria, whose husband has since died. She's all alone now with four children to support, but I've been sending her small sums of money through Carmelita. (Please don't tell your father—I told him I wanted a new outfit, and I did buy myself a pretty dress, but it cost next to nothing. Peanuts, compared to the fortune I used to spend on clothes. It shames me to think how much money I've wasted over the years. One piece of my jewelry could feed and house a family like Maria's for ages!)

    I hope you don't mind my writing at such length and so

often. I feel that you're the only person who could possibly understand. I've been a child. No, worse than a child. Children are honest, aren't they? They can't help but tell the truth. I've been lying to myself for years, pretending to be the person everybody wanted me to be. A plaything made of cardboard like one of Cara's paper dolls. Dress me up and take me anywhere.

Well, I'm through with that life! I can be my own person, like Diego. I will not let your father or anyone else tell me what to do or how to behave.

As ever,
Vivien

Walden Lodge
September 16, 1942
Darling Gray,

I'm sorry if my last letter gave you cause for concern. Please don't worry about me. I'm not despondent at all. Quite the opposite. I'm filled with energy these days. For one thing, I'm trying to educate myself about politics. Geoffrey has drawn up a list of books for me to read and I've diligently been working my way through them. He's been very patient, considering how ignorant I am (you know I never finished high school), but I fear that I'm not a very good student. People like you and Geoffrey may find answers in books, but I need to see things with my own eyes.

So here's my exciting news. I ran into a girlfriend from my Metro days, Delores Moore. We were in a couple of pictures together, and I knew that she'd gotten married to Bernie Herbert, a writer at MGM (did you know him?). They have two children and she's given up acting, but she writes stories for magazines. And she knows people. The same people you know. I won't say more, darling, except that it's very exciting. I feel use-ful, for the first time in my life.

> *As ever,*
> *Vivien*

My mother wanted to be useful. Reading that final sentence of hers, I felt connected to Vivien in a new way. I saw her, finally, as a person in her own right, someone not so very different from me. Ever since I'd come back from Italy, I'd been adrift, moping about the house in Hampstead Heath wondering what to do. Gray was hard at work on a new play, huddled over his Olivetti, a new model he'd bought himself with the proceeds from *Out of Place* that he was very proud of. Even Fog kept herself busy mousing at night, and sleeping it off during the day.

I missed Italy. It wasn't the work itself—the acting, I mean—but the camaraderie I missed, being part of a production, build-ing the film piece by piece, each of us doing our part. Take away any one component and the enterprise would still exist. A single actor or cameraman could be replaced; much as he'd hate to hear it, not even Luca was indispensable, although his vision did serve to unite us. But in the end, we'd created something grand. I sensed that this was the sort of usefulness that Vivien wanted.

I turned my attention back to her final letter.

Walden Lodge
October 8, 1942
Darling Gray,

   How marvelous that you will soon be back in Los Angeles, and not stationed all the way across the country. I hope that you'll have time to visit us at the lodge when you get here, but I should probably warn you that your father is not very happy with me. I've told him I don't want to star in his new picture.

He thinks people want an escape from all the horrible events of the war. The movies are where they go to put aside their problems and dream a little. What's wrong with being the woman they dream about? he says.

I'll tell you what's wrong, because I've tried to tell him, but he refuses to listen. I'm tired of it, darling. I'm tired of roles where all that's required of me is that I bat my eyelashes at the leading man and look good in an evening gown. I'm tired of playing the sweetheart and the girl next door. That's all your father sees in me, and I can't get him to understand that I'm not the seventeen-year-old ninny he married.

You know, I get bags full of letters from soldiers now. The studio responds to each and every one, as part of the war effort. Keeps up the morale of the troops. They've got a girl who signs my name to photos all day. The one they're using is a publicity still from Lace and Lilacs, *where I'm wearing a frilly dress and smiling at William Bright (although he's been cropped out of the scene, so all you see is me, with a come-hither look in my eye.) I asked them to use a different photo. I had one taken, in Mexico, with some of the Mexican ladies who worked on the set. We're standing together, sharing a smoke. I'm in costume and full makeup, and we look like sisters. That's how I want our boys in uniform to see me, as one of them, one of the people. I'm sending you a copy, and I'll even sign it myself.*

But listen, darling. What would you say if I were to meet you some evening in Culver City? I'd so love to talk to you privately about the work I've been doing with our mutual friends.

I do look forward to having you nearby.

As ever,
Vivien

"What is it, Cara?"

I pulled myself out of a reverie to find Gray regarding me with concern. The hotel pianist was playing "Begin the Beguine," and I realized that I'd been humming it under my breath as I was reading. A memory surfaced of Vivien humming the song as she spritzed herself with perfume in her dressing room. She often hummed at her toilette, and sometimes, if I knew the song, I'd sing the words.

"That song," I started to say, but the sentence stuck in my throat. She'd been happy—I remembered times she was happy with me. The two of us, together in her boudoir, me watching as she applied her makeup, me helping her with her zipper. I'd been there with her at home during the entire period when she was writing to Gray, but in her letters there was more mention of Geoffrey than of me. It was as if I hadn't existed so far as she was concerned. I blinked, releasing a torrent of tears whose flow I attempted to staunch with a linen napkin. In a minute I was afraid I'd start blubbering, right there in Brown's Hotel, causing the very proper English ladies at the next table to regard me with disapproval.

"Ah, Cara. I was afraid of this," Gray said grimly. "Come on, kid. Let's get out of here."

The next thing I knew, he was at my side, helping me out of my chair, draping an arm around my shoulders, guiding me through the dining room and out to the pavement. We walked for several blocks along the quiet Mayfair streets as dusk fell and the air grew chilly. I pulled my sweater more tightly around me, refusing his loan of his overcoat. The cold gave me something to focus on, something external to distract me from the turmoil inside. Slowly I regained my equilibrium.

"This letter," I said, waving the topmost one from the packet I was clutching. "Was it the last?" I was hoping for more, I realized, because I still hadn't learned enough.

"The last one she wrote to me in New Jersey, do you mean? Yes, it was. I was stationed in Los Angeles for the remainder of the war—that's where the Motion Picture Unit was—so I was able to see her after that. I saw you, too. Several times. I came up to the lodge in my uniform when I had leave, do you remember? You didn't recognize me at first."

I searched my memory, but the only image of Gray in military garb that I could recall was when he was one of the coffin bearers at Vivien's funeral. I took a breath and asked another question to blot that image out.

"Did you meet her in private as well?" I said.

He nodded.

"What did you talk about?"

"Politics, mostly."

"Didn't she ever talk about me?" It sounded pathetic, but I had to ask. So much about her own activities, her hopes and frustrations, and yet I'd been there the whole time.

"I'll tell you the truth, Cara," he said, stopping to face me on the sidewalk. "Your mother was like a woman possessed, the times I saw her. A convert to a new religion couldn't have been more single-minded in her devotion, or more deluded. Once she joined the Party, all she wanted to talk about was her Hollywood cell. The debates they got into, the activities they were planning. I couldn't get a word in edgewise. More than once I told her she was playing with fire, but she wouldn't listen. It was all too intoxicating. The secret meetings, running risks . . ."

"Wait a minute," I interrupted. "Are you saying that she was in danger?" I remembered the photo of the "mysterious man." Maybe he'd been a Soviet spy who'd decided she knew too much and had her snuffed out. Or an undercover agent the FBI'd put on her tail.

Gray made a dismissive motion with his hand. "I doubt the Soviets would have been interested in your mother. As for the FBI, everyone suspected that they'd infiltrated the American Communist Party. They had agents everywhere, but they were so transparent. I was teaching a course on screenwriting after the war, at the League of American Writers school. They were on the left, although not doctrinaire. The Marxists were all in the People's Education Center. But I'm convinced a couple of my students were FBI agents. You could tell they cared nothing about film, or writing, but they were always taking notes."

"So she might have been murdered!"

"I don't think so." I could see him weighing his words in an effort to spare my feelings. "Look," he said, clasping my cold hands in his warm ones. "Vivien had a strong sense of justice. It bothered her when she realized how unfair the world was, and, like many of us in those days, she was drawn into the movement that seemed to be committed to righting wrongs and standing up for the rights of others. Also like many of us, she was deceived. After all she'd invested in this new religion of hers, I'm afraid it might have been difficult for her to accept that she'd been left with nothing. She so wanted to feel needed."

"I don't understand." I felt more tears welling up in my eyes. Angrily, I swiped at them with the side of my hand. "I needed her, and she left me."

"She didn't leave you, Cara," he said gently. "She was lost."

My mother longed for something to give her life meaning, something more than the adulation of her fans and even—how it hurt to acknowledge this—the love of her husband and of her only child. Although he was too kind to say it outright, Gray thought she'd drowned herself after losing faith in her political ideals and, if I took myself out of the equation, I had an easier time understanding her unhappiness. You don't value what comes without effort. Who was Vivien Grant when she wasn't on the screen? She was twenty-seven years old before she asked herself this question, and was still trying to answer it when she

died. Twenty-seven! Her entire life was ahead of her, and yet
she chose to end it? I couldn't understand how she gave up so
easily on herself.

Vivien's letters were not the only gift my brother gave me for
my twenty-third birthday. When we got home, he presented me
with a book: *The Prophet*, by Kahlil Gibran.

"I read this in college—it was all the rage," he said. "I hadn't
thought about it in years, but the other day I saw a copy in the
window of a bookshop. I hope you like it."

The book had a yellow cover and printed beneath the title
was a drawing of the author's face. His eyes were in shadow,
giving the portrait an inward-turning feel. Leafing through the
slender volume, which seemed to be a collection of poetic reflec-
tions on a variety of topics, with strange drawings interspersed
among the verses, my eye was caught by a line in the section on
work.

"Oh, this is lovely!" I said. "Just listen: 'When you work you
are a flute through whose heart the whispering of the hours
turns to music.' And this: 'Work is love made visible.' "

"Work is love made visible," Gray murmured. "Yes, I
remember that one."

I scanned to the bottom of the page and continued reciting
Gibran's words until I reached the end of the stanza:

> "And what is it to work with love?
> "It is to weave the cloth with threads drawn from
> your heart,
> "even as if your beloved were to wear that cloth.
> "It is to build a house with affection,
> "even as if your beloved were to dwell in that
> house.
> "It is to sow seeds with tenderness and reap the
> harvest with joy,

"even as if your beloved were to eat the fruit.

"It is to charge all things you fashion with a
      breath of your own spirit,

"And to know that all the blessed dead

"are standing about you and watching."

When I finished reading, neither of us spoke for a long moment. "That's what you did, isn't it? When you wrote the play for Dory?"

"Yes," he said, clearing his throat. "That's what I did." He planted a kiss on my cheek. "Happy birthday, Cara."

CHAPTER ELEVEN:
CANNES
FRENCH RIVIERA, APRIL-MAY 1956

I hadn't seen Father since he'd put us on the train in Los
Angeles, and I'm not sure I'd ever paid attention to his physical
appearance. He'd been a fleeting presence in my life when I was
small, and once I started boarding school I only saw him at
Christmas and in the summers. In five years he'd become an
old man.

Geoffrey did try to prepare me. He and Father were already
in Cannes when I arrived, ensconced in their suite at the Carlton Hotel, resting up for the wedding. THE wedding, I should
say: Grace Kelly and Prince Rainier of Monaco. They'd
scheduled the event to take place right before the film festival,
so the Hollywood people would come.

Geoffrey opened the door and did a double-take when he
saw me. "Cara, child. Just look at you!"

"Do you like it?" I'd cut my hair in a pixie like Audrey Hep-
burn before setting off for the Côte d'Azur and was still trying
to decide whether it suited me.

"*Très chic*," Geoffrey pronounced. His gaze took in my new
outfit: a traveling suit not unlike the one I'd worn as Sylvia, a
black pillbox hat with veil, and a vanity case by Louis Vuitton.
"But where's the rest of your luggage?"

"I left it with the concierge. They'll have someone bring it up
when my room is ready—I'm just down the hall."

"Spiffing!" he said, ushering me into the suite. I looked
around the sumptuous sitting room, the oriental rugs, gilt-

framed still lifes on the walls, the antique tables upon which sat crystal vases filled with fresh-cut flowers. A cart bearing the remains of a room service breakfast was parked by the brocade sofa, its contents barely touched. I claimed a croissant for my own breakfast. I'd come directly from the train station and was famished.

"Where's Father?" I said through a mouthful of croissant. Flaky bits of pastry tumbled from my lips onto the carpet as I talked.

Geoffrey handed me a white linen napkin. "He's still in bed. It was a rough crossing and he found it rather debilitating, I'm sorry to say. Last night I asked the hotel doctor to give him something, to help him sleep."

"It seems to have done the trick," I observed, wiping crumbs from my lips. My watch said that it was nearly ten o'clock.

"I should warn you," said Geoffrey, lowering his voice. "He's been poorly, even before this trip, which I advised him not to make, if you must know. His heart is failing, and he's aware that he doesn't have much time left." He shook his head. "I'm afraid he took the news about your brother's passport complications rather hard. He was so hoping to see you both."

When Father called to invite us to Cannes for the wedding and the film festival, Gray was forced to tell him that he couldn't attend. The American government had refused to renew his passport, and it was only through the good graces of the British Home Office that he'd been allowed to stay in England.

"I can't enter France without a passport," he said. "You know they'd waste no time in deporting me back to the United States, and the minute that happens, I'd be in jail."

I'd known Father was disappointed, because Geoffrey phoned a day or two later in an attempt to persuade Gray to abandon his scruples and testify. I'd been out on a television audition when the conversation took place—I wasn't having much luck getting back into theater—but found my brother still fuming about it when I returned.

"Can you believe it? He told me to 'name a few insignificant names'!" said Gray in an impeccable imitation of our friend's Oxbridge accent. His voice grew bitter. "I always suspected he'd testified. I wonder how many poor suckers he fingered. Given the degree of his involvement in the Communist Party, the ranks were probably decimated by the time he finished."

"He actually admitted to testifying?" The revelation had dismayed me as well. I always saw Geoffrey as above the fray, unfocused perhaps, but highly principled. Committed to something nobler than saving his own skin. Out of solidarity with my brother, I offered to stay back in England.

"Nonsense!" Gray said. "Of course you're going. The hell with Geoffrey! Ignore him. You're doing this for Father and I'd join you in a heartbeat if I could. Three weeks on the French Riviera. Just imagine all the films you'll get to see, surrounded by film stars from around the world! And the royal wedding in Monaco: icing on the cake! I'll expect a full report when you get back."

As happy as Father was to see me (hugging for the first time, we both cried a little), the evidence of his decline was painfully obvious. If I'd passed him on the street, I might not have recognized him, so stooped and frail had he become, all the light gone from his eyes. He was sixty-four, but you'd have taken him for someone much, much older. I felt guilty for having stayed away so long; I could have gone back to the lodge for a visit, at least. In my eagerness to flee the place that held so many sad memories, the loss of my mother and my baby, I'd left him without a backward glance. Now I vowed to make it up to him while there was still time.

We spent most of the day sitting on the balcony, catching up. The sun was warm, and the sea glittered invitingly beyond the

Promenade de la Croisette, the curving boulevard some six floors below. I told him about my adventures in Sicily, beginning with the filming of *Stolen Love,* then skipping ahead to the story of Donald and La Normanna, the pilgrimage with Francesca to see Padre Pio, our visit to Rudolph Valentino's birthplace, and my encounter with the Gypsies on the beach. Luca's name was vaguely familiar, although he hadn't seen any of the Italian director's films. Father's tastes were entirely conventional.

"But tell me, Carissa," he said when I got to the part with the Fata Morgana. "Did that actress woman—"

"Francesca."

"All right, Francesca. Did she really leave you all alone in some godforsaken town in the middle of the night, putting you at the mercy of a band of Gypsies?"

With dismay, I realized that my account had alarmed him. The thought of his daughter abandoned in a foreign country with barely a cent, and more than a day's drive from the nearest American embassy, was Father's idea of a nightmare. My effort to entertain him had backfired, although he had laughed at how Francesca and I had disguised ourselves as widows, and at the tale of how she'd charmed *signore* Bardi. I hadn't intended to tell him about Valentino—I hadn't even told Gray—but I saw that the only way I could calm his fears was to distract him.

"Do you want to know how I was rescued?" I launched into the story of my encounter with Valentino, leaving out the business about my period, and downplaying Francesca's hysteria. The way I described it, the tarantella scene was little more than a charming folk dance, the Gypsies just one happy-go-lucky community who happened to like camping out on the beach. When I reached the point of the story where Valentino said goodbye and I drove off with Francesca in the Alfa, Father gave me a shrewd glance.

"He sounds like a gentleman," he commented.

"A gentleman?" The word didn't do him justice. To call someone a gentleman implied politeness, old-world manners, surface charm, but Valentino's kindness went well beyond this, and I sensed its source lay deep within. I struggled to come up with a description that wouldn't sound overblown. "He had a way of making you feel safe, like nothing bad could happen if you were with him."

"You're quite smitten with this fellow," Father observed matter-of-factly.

I gave a shrug and looked out across the harbor, to where the tall ships were moored. "Is it that obvious?"

"My dear child, it's nothing to be ashamed of!"

I kept my eyes fixed on the sea, afraid that if I met his eyes again, I'd divulge everything. More than once, I'd found myself fantasizing about going back to southern Italy to look for him. Once I got to Trani, I'd have no difficulty finding Guido's shop. I felt sure he'd be willing to tell me where Valentino lived. I pictured myself showing up on his doorstep. Would he be happy to see me? He'd called me "dearest." Surely he didn't call every girl "dearest" and touch her cheek while gazing longingly into her eyes.

"I thought that only happened in the movies," I said. "Falling in love at first sight."

Father reached over and patted my arm. "Don't give up on a Hollywood ending, Carissa."

The next morning was the royal wedding, and the three of us set off for Monaco in a hired Citroën. Our driver wove the car along the twisty mountain roads with great skill, but the trip proved tiring for Father. He dozed through much of the church ceremony, and we only stayed at the palace reception long enough for him to go through the receiving line and congratulate the new princess, whom he'd known early in her Hollywood career.

Everything about the wedding was magnificent, from the Monaco Cathedral itself, with its soaring arches, the light pouring in through the stained glass windows, to the altar beneath the gold mosaic dome where the priest read a blessing from the Pope. I'll never forget the sight of the beautiful Grace Kelly as she entered the nave, wearing the most exquisite silk gown, its lace bodice embroidered with hundreds and hundreds of seed pearls and on her head a crown of flowers holding in place a simple white tulle veil.

Of course, we saw dozens of stars at the reception. Gloria Swanson greeted Father like an old friend, although I could see from her expression that she too was dismayed by his haggard appearance.

"Ah, Robbie!" Cary Grant clasped my father's shoulder, then turned his handsome smile toward me. He looked better in a tuxedo than any other actor I'd ever seen. "Don't tell me this is little Cara. But where's that son of yours?"

Father gave a sad shake of his head but said nothing. I so wished Gray were there. On the ride back, I imagined telling him about the event, outlining my impressions to fix them in my memory. The wedding was spectacular from start to finish, and yet something nagged at me. The way her serene highness moved among her guests: it was all a performance, and as such it was flawless. The best of Grace Kelly's career. But wouldn't she eventually tire of being a princess, I wondered, the way Vivien had grown bored with her glamorous movie star persona? The noble but embittered wife of the drunk playwright she played in *The Country Girl,* the role that earned her an Oscar, allowed her far greater range than her current role as wife to a prince. I didn't envy her the fairy-tale marriage one bit, I decided, although I pretended otherwise with Geoffrey, just to get his goat.

"Admit it," I teased. "She had more class than Queen Elizabeth."

"Dear girl, there's no comparison between a film star and Her Royal Highness."

"Don't act as if you weren't as captivated as I was. I saw the way you gaped at her when she walked down the aisle on her father's arm."

Geoffrey gave a snort of protest. "I'm quite sure I was not gaping," he said. "I never gape." He paused to light a cigarette and offered the pack to me. I shook my head no. "The bride was stunning, I'll grant you that. But what kind of royalty marries an American *arriviste*, I ask you? Her father was an Irishman who made his fortune in bricks, I've read! A bricklayer's daughter the consort of the Prince of Monaco? A bricklayer's grandchildren on the throne?" He gave a dismissive shudder and took a long drag from his cigarette. "As I said, Cara child, there's no comparison."

Throughout this exchange, Father had been resting, eyes closed, with his elbow on the armrest, chin supported by his palm. We'd both assumed he was asleep, but apparently he'd been following the conversation, because he took Geoffrey to task for this diatribe.

"I thought you'd turned your back on all that hereditary aristocratic nonsense! I'm the son of a Hungarian tailor, as you well know, but you've been perfectly content to live off me for all these years."

"But, but . . ." Geoffrey spluttered, uncharacteristically at a loss for words. Nervously, he stubbed out his cigarette in the car's ashtray, but almost immediately lit another. I noticed his fingers shaking as he struck the match.

Father proceeded undeterred. "Why, I can remember when you called yourself a socialist. A Fabian, wasn't it? Between the wars. You weren't such a snob in those days." I noticed that Geoffrey was growing more uncomfortable by the minute. "Yes, I'm quite sure you gave me some of their pamphlets. What was the name of that couple? Webb, wasn't it? Sidney and Beatrice Webb. Couldn't get through any of that rubbish!"

"Was this what you gave my mother to read?" I interrupted.

A startled expression crossed Geoffrey's face. "Your mother?"

"You lent her books about Communism."

"I'm sure I did nothing of the sort! Your poor mother was a lovely woman, but she had no head for politics."

"Yes, I know. She did say you were very good to put up with her ignorance."

"She said *what?* But how . . . Wait a minute," he said, the new cigarette smoldering all but forgotten in his hand with two inches of ash. "How could you possibly claim to know something like this? You were a child at the time!"

Father rose to my defense. "You'd be surprised what children notice and remember. Particularly when it involves someone they love," he added quietly, a sorrowful look on his face.

I reached for his hand and squeezed it. "Actually, it's not something I remember," I said hurriedly, eager to change the subject. "Vivien wrote to Gray during the war. He showed me the letters, and in one of them she talked about how Geoffrey was teaching her about Communism."

This was clearly news to Father, who turned to face Geoffrey and said sharply, "You were?" Geoffrey muttered something to the effect that he'd only done as he was asked and that Vivien had not proven to be a very good student. Father glared at him a moment before turning to me and asking in a gentler voice, "Do you have those letters with you?"

I nodded. I'd brought them to read on the trip, along with *The Prophet*.

"But this is slanderous!" Geoffrey said. "Your mother was

telling people that I was indoctrinating her?"

"She wasn't telling *people*," I corrected him. "She told Gray, in a letter, and as far as I know I'm the only person he's shown it to. She hardly talked about you at all, if you want the truth. She mostly talked about herself and her Communist friends."

"I'd like to see those letters," said Father. "If you don't mind sharing them with me, that is."

"Are you sure?" I hated the thought of adding to his misery. There were things in those letters he might find troubling and I deeply regretted having brought up the subject.

"Listen to the child," agreed Geoffrey. He discovered the cigarette dangling from his hand and took a long puff, sprinkling ashes all over his trousers. "She has a point. Why dredge up that sorry old history?"

"I'll let Cara be the judge, I think," said Father, his tone mild but unyielding. "I'd like to know what my wife was up to in the final months of her life. Surely I deserve some insight, after all these years."

I showed Father the letters that same evening. We'd finished our meal in the marble-columned dining room and had parted with Geoffrey in the lobby. He was off to visit the hotel's casino, he informed us.

"If you lose your shirt, don't come running to me for a loan," quipped Father.

"Not to worry," Geoffrey said breezily. "A good gambler knows when to cut his losses."

"I wouldn't call him a good gambler," said Father as we made for the elevators. He let himself into his suite while I went to get Vivien's letters from my room. I was prepared to leave him alone to read them in peace, but Father patted the sofa cushion next to him.

"I'd like it if you stayed," he said.

I picked up the copy of the day's *New York Herald Tribune* that was lying on the coffee table and attempted to read the stories on the front page, but I kept glancing over to get a look at Father's face. He'd finish a letter and lay it on the cushion, and I'd try and see which one it was without being too obvious. Then he'd stare off into space for several minutes before he picked up the next letter. He took a very long time to get through the entire packet. Some of the letters he read more than once, and I'd given up the pretense of reading the paper well before he put the last letter down. For a long time he did not speak, as if trying to master his emotions before he opened his mouth.

"This is all?" he asked at last.

"Yes. Gray told me that he and Vivien met a number of times once he was back in L.A."

"Really? I didn't realize they'd been in contact. They never got along." Removing his wire-rimmed glasses, he rested his forehead on his hands. "But, of course. That explains it," he said to himself. "Oh, my dear. I misjudged your mother terribly . . ."

"You don't have to tell me this," I said, busying myself with the letters, folding each one and carefully replacing it in its envelope before returning the packet to my handbag. After all this time, it hardly mattered to me whether Father had misjudged Vivien or she'd misjudged him. No doubt there'd been misunderstanding on both sides, as in any relationship. In my short time with Adrian, I'd seen how silence could build to the point where the damage was beyond repair.

"I want to tell you, Carissa. I owe it to you, before I'm gone, to explain the circumstances surrounding your mother's death. I had her followed, you see. I wanted to find out where she was going, all those evenings she claimed to be attending meetings. I was jealous of anything that took her away from me, convinced there had to be a man at the bottom of it, one of those radicals she was always running off to see. And it was mostly men in those groups of hers."

I couldn't keep the shock and disapproval from my voice. "You had my mother followed?"

"I hired a detective, yes. It was wrong of me," Father agreed. "Very wrong."

I shook my head, not trusting myself to speak. I didn't want to know the things I was learning. What good would it do, going back over my parents' marital problems? Whatever Vivien had done, whatever mistakes Father had made, reliving the past wouldn't give me my mother back. If anything, reconstructing the events leading up to her death had estranged us; in coming to see my mother as a person in her own right, I'd lost her completely.

"It doesn't matter, Father," I managed to say, but he seemed intent on telling me everything.

"The night she drowned herself, we'd had a terrible argument, Carissa. I knew she'd met someone that very afternoon. My man followed her to a bar and he described the encounter. And it wasn't the first time he'd seen her with this fellow. There was no question in my mind that she was carrying on an affair, and I confronted her after you were in bed. Naturally, she denied everything, but I knew she was lying. I lost my temper, and threatened to divorce her. I meant it too. I told her I'd produce evidence of adultery in court, enough to prove her unsuitability as a mother. I used you against her . . ." Here he broke down completely, wrenching sobs torn from his lungs. "I was so enraged, I dragged her to the door, threw her out into the night in her negligee, and locked the house. I drove your poor mother to her death. And now I see that the entire thing was in my head. She was meeting your brother! Please forgive me, Carissa."

It was too much to absorb, this new information. I'd need to sit with it, all by myself. Maybe in time I'd come to blame Father for his part in Vivien's death, but I doubted it. At that moment I felt sorry for him. The sight of his torment, after all these years, the dreadful secret he'd been keeping, brought me to tears as well.

"It's not your fault, it's not your fault," I kept repeating as the tears coursed down my cheeks. Eventually we managed to comfort one another, and I wouldn't leave until I'd ordered us tea and stayed long enough to drink a cup with him before seeing him settled in bed. I kissed him on the top of the head, turned off the lights in his suite, and went down the corridor to my own room, but I was much too restless to stay indoors. Fetching a wrap from my closet, I went downstairs and out through the lobby, to walk along the promenade.

She loved me after all. The realization came with the first scent of the ocean breeze as I stepped through the revolving doors. Gray was right that Vivien had taken her own life, but he was wrong about her motives. It wasn't disillusionment with her political ideals that drove her to drown herself, it was despair over the prospect of losing me. Of course I mourned her all the more, knowing this, but an ancient grief had been lifted from my soul. *She loved me. She loved me.* I wandered among the nighttime pedestrians on the Boulevard de la Croisette, hearing their noise and laughter the way you hear sounds underwater. Muted and distorted, bursts of conversation like bright fish at the edge of my awareness, too fleeting to catch. I floated on a tide of Vivien's love past the nightclubs and cafés, beneath palm trees lit silvery blue in the streetlights. Jewelry-laden women in elegant evening gowns strolled past from the opposite direction on the arms of men in tuxedos, traffic surged in the street as the lights changed. I moved along at the pace of the other walkers, turning back as they did when we reached one end of the promenade and wandering the other way, giddy with relief.

As midnight approached, I returned to the Carlton. I should have been exhausted after the day's exertion, but I wasn't. Perhaps it would help if I took a long bath, I was thinking as I walked through the lobby and headed to the elevators. But then I heard a familiar woman's voice demanding, in Italian, that she be given a different room.

"Subito," she was saying. Right away. Her back was to me as she argued with the desk clerk, but there was no mistaking that regal tone.

"Francesca?" I was still some distance away, and her attention was focused on the clerk. I strode across the lobby and tapped her on the shoulder. The actress turned her head, her initial expression of confusion giving way to sheer happiness as she recognized me with my new haircut.

"Carissima!" She threw her arms around my neck and kissed me forcefully several times on each cheek. "How wonderful to see you here! I should have phoned you in England. We have so much to talk about. And I owe you an apology too, for leaving you on the side of the road. I was not right in the head."

"Scusi, signora . . ." The clerk attempted to get her attention.

"Un attimo." She turned back to face the man, putting him in his place. "Can't you tell I'm busy?" Seeing her in profile, I noticed that she was not as trim as she used to be. Her belly bulged, and her breasts seemed to be spilling out of her low-cut top.

"Francesca! You're not expecting!"

The actress laughed, tossing back her hair and jutting out her hip like one of the Gypsy women on the beach, proudly displaying her round belly. *"Si, si.* It was a miracle, *carissima."*

"A miracle," echoed Luca, who had come up behind us and was now embracing me with gusto.

"But how?" My voice came out muffled as I was still crushed

against the director's chest.

"Padre Pio . . ." Francesca began to say, but Luca cut her off.

"My wife left me for her accountant."

The actress showed me her left hand, upon which glittered a good-sized diamond ring. "We're getting married as soon as his marriage is annulled."

"Oh, Francesca! It's beautiful! Congratulations!"

Luca insisted on celebrating our reunion in style. A discreet handover of francs, and a penthouse suite miraculously became available. A fleet of bellhops assembled to take Luca and Francesca's luggage upstairs and the three of us made our way to a table in the bar, where Luca ordered an expensive bottle of champagne.

"Here's to miracles!" I said, toasting the happy couple.

"This one is costing me a pretty penny," Luca grumbled, draining his glass and pouring himself another.

"What are you complaining about?" Francesca admonished him. "His wife's new husband is rich," she confided to me. "He's getting off cheap."

"Of course he's rich. He was my accountant too, the dirty thief!"

Champagne always goes straight to my head. After one glass, Francesca wished us goodnight, leaving Luca and me to finish the bottle by ourselves. I learned about the director's current project, a film about prostitutes set in Palermo—La Normanna had evidently been a great source of inspiration—but I must have finally succumbed to my fatigue because whatever else we talked about is forever lost in a fizzy haze.

I woke up in my own bed the next day, nicely tucked in, shoes off, and with no memory of how I'd gotten there. A long bath and several aspirin washed down with coffee, and I finally felt fit enough to venture down the hallway and say good morning to Father. Geoffrey opened the door and motioned me into the suite, a finger on his lips, cautioning me to silence.

"What is it? What's wrong?" I asked in a worried whisper.

"He's had a fall. I found him on the floor. The doctor's in with him now."

From the bedroom, we heard Father calling to us in a tremulous voice. "Cara? Is that you? Geoffrey? Is Cara with you?"

"I'm here, Father," I said, coming to stand in the doorway of his room. He was propped up in bed, looking pale and disheveled, an ugly gash on the left side of his forehead. The hotel doctor, a middle-aged man with a salt-and-pepper beard, was tending to the wound. When he'd finished cleaning it and bandaging Father's head, he beckoned me to the bedside.

"You are the daughter? He needs to go to the hospital for tests. I have told him this already. Perhaps you will persuade him, Miss Walden?" he appealed, his English betraying the faintest trace of a French accent.

Father scowled at him. "I don't need tests to tell me what I already know!"

"The doctor knows more than you do," I said in a placating tone. "At the hospital they might be able to figure out what's been making you so tired and weak."

"It's called old age, and there's no cure for it."

The doctor shook his head and began packing up his bag. "He is a stubborn man, your father."

"Don't you want to feel better?" I persisted. "I'm sure there's medicine you could take, once they find out what's wrong with you. You can't just give up like this."

"Medicine!" he scoffed. But then his voice softened. "Having you here with me, Carissa, is the only medicine I need."

★　★　★　★　★

Geoffrey and I escorted Father to the gala opening of the film festival, and we all attended the screening of the award-winning documentary by Jacques Cousteau, *The Silent World*. From the opening shots of the divers descending into the sea, brandishing flares as they fell deeper and deeper into the dark blue realms, aqualungs strapped to their backs, the three of us were captivated. When they reached a certain depth, the five "menfish" shone floodlights on the underwater scenery, and we were treated to a dazzling display of orange and red coral reefs.

"Splendid!" said Father, clearly enjoying the spectacle. Unfortunately, the spectacle of the film festival itself was too much for him. The crowds of celebrities and paparazzi, the noise and chaos everywhere we went, left him so drained we didn't dare venture out with him again. Geoffrey and I took turns after that, one going to the theater while the other kept Father company. He seemed content to sit on the balcony for long periods in the late morning, reading the paper or drowsing in a lounge chair. For lunch, I'd tempt his appetite with fresh fruit and cheese; for dinner, all he'd take was consommé and some biscuits soaked in Marsala—an old Italian remedy suggested by Francesca. I'd invited her and Luca up to the suite one afternoon and of course she'd captivated him, the way she'd captivated Luca's guests at the villa.

"I do believe she was flirting with me!" he told me later, pleased as punch.

"Lucky for you Luca's liberal minded," I said. "Otherwise he might have challenged you to a duel."

A twinkle came into Father's eye, a flicker of his old self. "Do you know, I once fought a man for a woman's favors in Paris? This was years before I met your mother," he assured me.

"Who was she? Some famous beauty?" I pictured a glamorous 1920s French actress; Father was quite handsome in his younger days.

"Oh, nothing so grand as that. She was, er"—he blushed—"a courtesan."

"Do tell," said Geoffrey, looking up from *Les Misérables*. He'd bought himself a fine edition of Victor Hugo's works with his winnings—he'd apparently done quite well the other evening—and had been haunting the casinos most nights since then, generally not returning until the wee hours of the morning.

Father chuckled. "There isn't much more to tell. I lost and she went off with the other fellow. We fought outside a café on the Champs Elysées, not far from the George V, as I recall."

"Perhaps we should commission a commemorative plaque," Geoffrey said, lighting up a cigarette and going out on the balcony to smoke. I joined him and lit one of my own, a Gitane. Being in France, I couldn't resist.

"Don't you think we should arrange for a nurse to accompany us on the trip home?" I'd made up my mind to return with Father and Geoffrey to California, and had cabled Gray to let him know. He'd called me later that same day, full of questions about Father's condition, and that night he and Father spoke on the phone for a very long time.

Geoffrey did not answer immediately. I blew a smoke ring and had time to see it dissolve completely before he spoke. "The Hindus regard death as a natural part of the soul's journey. We can no more prevent it than we can stop the rain from falling or the earth from orbiting the sun."

"Yes, I know," I said impatiently. Geoffrey's lessons on Indian philosophy could go on forever. "But I don't want Father to suffer needlessly. You said he was uncomfortable on the voyage out."

"Life entails suffering, Cara child. The only way to end it is to loosen the bonds that attach us to this earth and rejoin the universal."

I didn't like the turn the conversation was taking. "So what are you proposing? Letting him die on the ship?" It was all I could do to keep my voice down, he sounded so heartless.

"I can think of worse things than a funeral at sea," said Geoffrey, taking a final draw of his cigarette and flicking it over the edge of the balcony. I watched it fall, lit end glowing bright, until it hit the pavement below.

CHAPTER TWELVE:
JAKUB

That evening, I went with Luca and Francesca to the screening of another French documentary, one that had provoked a great deal of controversy. *Night and Fog* was the name of the picture, and its subject was the Nazis' effort to exterminate the Jews. Gray and I had both read Anne Frank's diary, but terrible as that story was, it stopped short of describing what happened to her after she and her family were discovered in their hiding place. This picture picked up where the book left off.

The film was being shown in the main auditorium, where we'd seen the Cousteau documentary, but was not part of the official program. The German government had lodged a protest when the film was first nominated, Luca explained as we made our way to the venue, and the festival authorities had been obliged to remove it from the selection under pressure from the French Foreign Ministry. But after protests from a number of groups, including Communists, Resistance organizations, and Jewish survivors, it was announced that *Night and Fog* would be shown after all, but outside the competition.

I put a hand on Luca's forearm, to delay our entry into the theater. "Why were the Communists upset?" I understood the reactions of the Resistance members and Jews. They'd been deported to the concentration camps and suffered unimaginable atrocities. But it seemed as if Communists these days spent most of their time debating issues. They might have made revolutions in Russia and China, but they didn't seem to be doing much in Europe, I told him.

Francesca gave a barely perceptible shake of her head, but it was too late. "The Communists *were* the Resistance in France!" Luca exclaimed. "They took all the risks while de Gaulle's gang stayed safely in England. Thousands of them died in the camps. Thousands! Betrayed by other French people and arrested by the French police! Didn't you know this in America?"

Sheepishly, I admitted that I'd known nothing.

"How could she have known? She wasn't in the war," scolded Francesca, giving Luca a stern look. "Besides, she was a child when it happened."

"You are right, *amore*," he said. Turning to me, he gave a mock bow and begged my forgiveness.

"Forgiveness granted, *gentile signore*. But you weren't wrong to scold me for my ignorance," I said, thinking about Vivien. "I'm no longer a child and it's time I learned about events in the world."

"Brava!" said Luca.

Festival Hall was packed and we had difficulty finding seats together, but Luca succeeded in persuading a couple of people to shift places, freeing up a block of three seats midway down a row near the front of the auditorium. The lights were dimming as we picked our way around the other audience members and slid into our seats. Less than ten minutes into the documentary, Francesca grew so distraught at the shots of Jewish women and children being rounded up at gunpoint and herded onto trains that she asked Luca to take her back to the hotel.

"Are you sure you don't want to come with us, *carissima*?" she whispered. "You shouldn't be watching this all by yourself."

As terrible as the images were, I felt that it was important to stay. "Please don't worry about me," I whispered back. "I want to know."

I hardly noticed when they left, I was so shaken by the sight of the skeletal men behind barbed wire, wearing what looked like striped pajamas, and by the hollow look in their eyes. The still photos were awful enough, but the moving sequences were unbearable. Piles of bodies being bulldozed into a pit and covered with earth, grainy footage of the sick and dying, their faces etched with pain. The Nazis had filmed the subjects of their perverse medical experiments, along with the machinery they'd constructed to perform amputations and other cruel mutilations. They'd documented everything: the piles of shoes and eyeglasses taken from the dead and redistributed in Germany. The mountains of hair used to make cloth, the bones ground into fertilizer. Everything was saved, we were told by the dispassionate narrator, whose tone grew more accusatory as the film approached its conclusion. "We pretend it all happened only once, at a given time and place. We turn a blind eye to what surrounds us, and a deaf ear to humanity's never-ending cry."

How could the world have let it happen? I sat shivering in the darkness as the credits rolled, overwhelmed by the horror I'd seen. Too shaken to cry, I felt a scream mounting inside of me and I feared that if I opened my mouth, it would escape my lips and shatter the silence of the theater. I squeezed my eyes shut and covered my mouth with my hands, sensing the movement around me as the other patrons shuffled out, the murmured apologies as they made their way around those still seated.

When the lights came on, I realized that the row I was sitting in was nearly empty. Numbly, I surveyed the auditorium as I attempted to bring myself back into the present moment. Those audience members who'd stayed seemed stunned as well, staring at the now dark screen. Nobody spoke, although I heard the sound of people blowing their noses and clearing their throats. In the row ahead of me a young man sat alone, his hunched posture and the trembling of his shoulders making it apparent that he was weeping, but soundlessly. My heart went out to him, this stranger with his private grief. For some reason, I could not bring myself to leave him there by himself, in such anguish, and so I remained in my seat as the auditorium gradually emptied, thinking about the film and its bleak message, that the degradation of man by his fellow creatures is made possible by our willingness to look away.

"Vous êtes encore là! Mais, qu'est-ce vous faites, alors?" said the stranger, turning suddenly to face me. I didn't understand his rapid French, but his tone conveyed his anger clearly enough. I opened my mouth to apologize, trying to remember the words for "forgive me," but then I looked at his face and was at a loss for words in any language. I reached out a hand and touched Valentino's tear-stained cheek, seeing his eyes widen as he took in my changed appearance.

"It's you," he said, covering my hand with his own and pressing it tenderly against his face.

"Yes, it's me."

He lost everyone he'd ever loved. Some died in the Warsaw Ghetto, others in Treblinka. For years he lived in the shadow of these losses and wished that he had died along with them.

Jakub himself was in Paris studying violin at the Conservatoire when the war broke out. Poland fell, and he soon lost contact with his family. Then France fell and life became difficult for Jews in France as well. Schools were closed to them, and immigrants were being deported. Next came the roundups: thousands of Jews from all over France arrested and interned in various camps around the country. Most would end up in Auschwitz. At that point, Jakub made the decision to join the Resistance rather than go back to Poland, a decision he later regretted.

After the war he found one uncle, his father's kid brother

Arie, who told him what he knew about the fate of the others. The Nazis had instituted a quota system for the Ghetto: so many Jews delivered for deportation to "the East" every day. They gave the Jewish Council the task of selecting those to be deported, and Jakub's grandmother on his father's side was put on the first transport on account of her illness. Nobody believed the official explanation, that the old and infirm were being sent to the countryside for resettlement, but the truth was so incredible—unthinkable, really—that nobody wanted to believe it, either. Not Jakub's grandfather, who insisted on accompanying her, and he convinced Arie to allow his wife Mira to go as well. Mira was expecting their first child, and the Ghetto was no place for a pregnant woman. They were all starving, living on top of one another, entire families sharing a single apartment. Arie thought that she'd be better taken care of in the countryside and pushed her to leave with the others. How could he have known they'd be gassed immediately upon arrival, along with thousands of others?

Jakub's mother was rounded up while waiting in line for the family's bread ration. His father was shot when the Germans entered the Ghetto, together with another aunt and uncle and their three children, who were living with him. His younger sister, Bracha, belonged to the underground and was captured during the uprising. Bracha somehow managed to survive Majdanek. The Red Cross had gotten word to Jakub in Paris that she was in the Displaced Persons camp in Trani; the city was full of refugees from every corner of Europe, all trying to track down their relatives after the war, and the authorities were doing everything they could to reunite families. They'd found out where Bracha was and provided him with a train ticket to Bari, but so many of the lines in that part of Italy had been damaged in the bombing that it took him nearly two weeks to get there. By the time he arrived, his sister had succumbed to typhus. It was May, he said, and every spring he went back to lay a stone on her grave in the little cemetery the Italians had built for the Jews who'd died there. Over the years, he'd met others who'd been interned with his sister, including Guido's wife, who was also a Polish Jew.

"And the Gypsies?" I asked.

"The Gypsies were in the death camps too, and many were buried with Bracha."

We were walking along the beach, following the curve of shore that clung to the Cannes harbor. No words of mine could soothe his suffering or restore to him his murdered family, but I made a vow then and there, as we stood together in the dark. If he'd allow me to remain in his life, I'd do everything in my power to make him whole again.

In time, I'd learn his entire story. The lost months after Bracha's death, when he succumbed to grief in the DP camp in Italy, not caring whether he lived or died. Many of the Jews in the camp were making their way to Palestine. It was risky: the British refused to let Jews emigrate into the territory, which they still controlled. They'd set up a blockade to prevent the refugees' ships from entering the port of Haifa, and the ones they captured were sent to internment camps in Cyprus, but after what they'd been through, the refugees were undeterred. Jakub was tempted to join them and start his life over in the promised land. He'd heard the stories of the Polish survivors; on some level he knew he had nobody left, but in the end he made up his mind to go back to Warsaw and seek out whatever traces might remain of his family.

He went with the Gypsies, living as they did in makeshift camps and sleeping under the stars. He passed refugees traveling in both directions, ragged families driven from their homes, or returning to places that were no longer home. Slowly he worked his way up through Italy into Austria and Czechoslovakia with the troupe, bartering their services for a bit of food and playing their music at night. He liked it that they left him largely to his own devices. "I wasn't fit for human company," he would tell me.

He parted ways with his traveling companions when they reached Prague. The city had an office for Jewish refugees where he found other Poles, a number of whom had tried returning to their former homes, only to be met with violence. They warned him not to go on; Warsaw was in ruins and the authorities were doing everything in their power to drive Jews out. It wasn't safe for Jews in Poland after the war, but Jakub gave me to understand that he couldn't turn back. He had to know what happened to his family, and so he became someone else.

In the Resistance he'd gone about disguised as a seminary student, Claude Lassegue. He was very diligent, Claude was, working late nights, staying out after curfew. He kept a Bible in his satchel. Once when he got caught by the French police, he opened the Bible and read a passage to the gendarmes, right there in the prefecture. "They shall see who have never been told of him, and they shall understand who have never heard of him." Such an earnest young man, spreading the word of God. Jakub would admit that he grew very fond of him. And the habit of caution he'd learned in the underground served him well: in the black market in Prague, he got hold of a cassock and once more assumed the identity of Claude. In this guise, he returned to Warsaw.

Despite everything he'd been told, and even after all the destruction he'd witnessed on his journey through war-torn Europe, the sight of his city reduced to ruins shocked Jakub. He couldn't find his family's apartment building in the old Jewish quarter. His entire neighborhood, which had been within the boundaries of the Ghetto, had been leveled. All that remained in that deathly landscape were fragments: a wall here, a steeple there, blasted facades of once majestic buildings with nothing behind them, weeds growing where there had been sidewalks, scorched tree trunks and twisted metal posts marking the tram route through the district. I couldn't imagine the desolation when he told me, but later I'd see photos. The streets had been cleared of rubble and an odd assortment of vehicles could be found on the roads. Horse-drawn carts and battered buses drove alongside army jeeps and trucks delivering supplies to the city's residents; everything had to be brought in from outside.

Inhabiting another identity insulated Jakub from the surrounding devastation to some extent. In Claude's cassock he felt like an outsider, as he would explain, trying to understand it for himself, a stranger visiting an unfamiliar city that held no special meaning. But then he'd come upon a sight that triggered a childhood memory. It might be the slant of light on the Vistula, evoking a scene in his mind, a vision of a late summer afternoon spent strolling with his parents and sister along the banks of the river. His mother was wearing a new hat, a pert straw hat trimmed with ostrich feathers that she wore tilted to one side. She was very fashionable and subscribed to Paris fashion magazines to keep up with the latest styles. Twice a year she took Jakub and Bracha shopping at Jabłkowski Brothers, Warsaw's best department store.

After the war, Jabłkowski Brothers was being used as an aid depot, and it was there that Jakub was reunited with Arie. Winter was approaching. He'd been in Warsaw for several months already, living in a shelter, and the first time he didn't recognize his uncle. The man was hunched over a small fire in what had once been a park with several others, all of them apparently living on the streets. Jakub had paused nearby to light a cigarette and noticed the man staring at him in his priest's clothing. There was something discomfiting in the man's gaze and Jakub moved on quickly. He'd put the incident out of his mind—so many of the people he encountered had the same haunted expression, he would say—but a few weeks later the same man showed up at the aid depot. There was a wall where people would post messages addressed to missing relatives. Jakub was in the habit of checking the wall every few days, and that morning he heard someone speak his name.

"Abramowicz. Jakub Abramowicz." He would describe for me how he looked around, startled by the sound of his name, fearful that he'd been found out as an impostor, and saw the disheveled figure approaching from across the room. Not until the man was standing right in front of him did Jakub recognize Arie. His uncle took him back to the park and introduced him to the others—all that remained of a small band of fighters who'd managed to escape through the sewers after the Ghetto uprising. Before the war, Arie had taught in a Jewish high school that continued operating in secret when Jewish schools were closed after the German invasion. Jakub remembered him as a scholarly person, passionate about medieval philosophy, which had been his subject. A man more comfortable in the world of Maimonides than in his own era. Now he and his comrades were bent on revenge, hunting down those who had betrayed them and their loved ones and meting out what they called justice.

Maybe it had something to do with going about dressed as a priest, Jakub would speculate, but he had no desire for vengeance. "An eye for an eye, and the whole world would be blind," wrote Khalil Gibran. Jakub's uncle accused him of cowardice, but who was Arie to play God? With a heavy heart, he made his way back to Paris to finish his music studies, supporting himself by working as a monitor in a Jewish orphanage. On his nights off, he liked to go to the Latin Quarter to hear American jazz, and it wasn't long before he was playing gigs all over France, moving with the seasons from village concerts to the big festivals in resort cities. He prefers the smaller venues, my Jakub, but I've always had a soft spot for the Riviera because it was where we found one another again.

Father was asleep when I let myself into the suite, and Geoffrey was already off to the casinos. He'd left the windows open and the rooms felt clammy with the damp air blowing in off the sea. Fine for a man who went for a morning swim in any weather, but hardly proper for Father in his weakened condition. I went around pulling the windows shut, beginning with Father's bedroom, straightening his covers and listening for a few moments to the rise and fall of his breath. I latched the French doors in the living room and closed the drapes, then moved to secure the windows in Geoffrey's room, which were rattling in the breeze.

I used to like visiting Geoffrey's cabin at the lodge. You never knew what you'd find, tucked away behind some tome on his bookshelf or lying haphazardly on the floor. Next to a half-eaten sandwich on a Limoges china plate might be an Egyptian amulet he'd collected at some point on his travels, which he'd been studying over lunch. You'd pick up one of his shoes and find a gyroscope tucked inside, or a crystal goblet from Venice being used to hold pencils. The old thrill of discovery took hold of me when I entered his hotel bedroom and saw his latest purchases scattered about, the volumes of Hugo resting, spine-open, on various surfaces, a brocade dressing gown laid out on the bed, beside it a hand-tooled leather case containing a set of silver inlaid dueling pistols.

None of this loot was cheap. Either Geoffrey had taken up burgling our fellow guests' hotel rooms, like Cary Grant's nemesis in *To Catch a Thief,* or he'd developed his own system to plunder the casinos. In either case, I wondered how long it would be before he got caught.

But no, he wasn't the type to get caught. Even if he turned out to be stealing or gaming the system, he'd somehow manage to slip away. He'd act absent-minded, or he'd confess to his crimes with such disarming honesty that the whole thing would seem like a game. Either way, he'd be off the hook—and maybe he'd have succeeded in diverting attention from his own activities by implicating someone else.

It occurred to me that I could no longer trust Geoffrey. On the surface he seemed perfectly harmless, almost laughable with his arcane interests and mystical pretensions, but underneath I sensed a devious mind, always calculating its own advantages. I was glad I'd decided to go back to California with Father and, regardless of Geoffrey's opinion, I intended to hire a nurse to help me take care of him on the voyage home. With only three days remaining before we sailed, I'd have to scurry to make all the arrangements, which wouldn't leave me much time to spend with Jakub, but I'd told him all about Father on the walk that evening and felt sure he'd understand.

I was looking forward to introducing the two of them the next day. Imagining Father's surprise when I produced "Valentino" made me smile, but I was the one who was most surprised by how well the two of them hit it off. Father also surprised me by telling Jakub about his own childhood, growing up in a little town in the northeastern corner of Hungary, in the region where they made wine. He'd always been tight-lipped about his past, and I'd never thought to question him about the world he'd left behind. Now I learned that he'd been born into a moderately wealthy Jewish family, that he'd had a brother named Jákob, along with two sisters named Zsófia and Rose, and that his original last name was Szabó, which meant "tailor" in Hungarian.

There were so many things I didn't know. How could I have been so incurious? The sea crossing would give us time to talk, and I hoped to learn more about Father's life in Hungary. Of course, having seen *Night and Fog* and from the little I'd heard of Jakub's story, I was afraid of what I might learn about the fate of his sisters and brothers. I'd seen a cloud pass over his face when he'd mentioned them. I wouldn't press him, I decided. We'd take it slowly. But it was time I knew about my family history.

"Your brother's real name was Hungarian, too. Géza. A grand old Magyar name," Father said. "His mother chose it." He gave a little shake of the head.

"Really?" I couldn't believe I didn't know any of this. Jakub had learned more in ten minutes than I'd learned in my whole life.

"First day of school, he came home and told us he wanted an American name. He insisted that we speak English too. The other children must have been giving him a hard time."

"Naming himself after a boring color doesn't sound like much of an improvement," I pointed out. "I'll bet he still got beat up."

Father chuckled. "Oh, he called himself Jimmy in those days, but at Yale he became rather artistic and changed it to Gray."

"Jimmy!" I could barely contain my glee, imagining my brother's reaction when I called him by his self-devised nickname. "I wish Gray were here now," I said, voicing my thoughts aloud.

"Spiriting somebody into France isn't difficult," Jakub said thoughtfully. He turned to Father. "Do you have a photograph of your son, sir?"

Father sent me into the bedroom to fetch his wallet. He extracted a snapshot and handed it to Jakub. "What do you need it for?"

"I'll explain everything, I promise. Right now I need to make some arrangements. We don't have much time before you leave."

A few hours later, Jakub phoned from the lobby. He had something to show us, he said. Father was resting in his room, so I told him I'd meet him downstairs. Too impatient to wait for the elevator, I took the stairs, arriving breathless in the lobby—but the sight of my beloved would have taken my breath away in any event.

He was wearing a suit and carrying a small suitcase. I saw that he'd had a shave and a haircut since the morning, but it wasn't his clothes or his well-groomed appearance that struck me, it was the way his face lit up the moment I came into view.

"You look beautiful," he said, kissing me quite formally, once on each cheek, as if we were nothing more than close acquaintances. This was how people greeted one another in broad daylight in the lobby of the Carlton Hotel, he seemed to feel.

I smiled. "What's in the suitcase?"

He shook his head in lieu of answering. "Would you like to sit on the terrace?" he suggested, leading the way outdoors. We took a table off to one side, away from the other customers, and ordered coffee. While we waited for it to arrive, Jakub pulled an envelope out of his breast pocket and handed it to me. The envelope contained a French passport that looked somewhat the worse for wear. The name of its owner was handwritten in ink on the first page, and visible through a lozenge-shaped cut-out on the blue cover: Claude Lassegue.

"This was yours?"

"It used to belong to me, yes. But I no longer need it, so I'm lending it to someone else." Reaching across the table, he flipped the pages until he got to the one with the owner's photo. There, riveted to the page by its corners and embossed with a seal bearing the insignia of the French Republic, was a reduced version of the snapshot of Gray.

I laughed out loud as enlightenment dawned. "How did you do it?"

"Oh, it's just a skill I picked up, during the war." He lowered his voice and glanced casually around, to make sure none of the other patrons were looking. Then Jakub told me his plan. He'd already booked a flight for himself from Cannes to London at eight p.m., and a flight back first thing the next morning for himself and a companion. All I had to do was to call the house in Hampstead and explain the whole thing to Gray. He'd take care of the rest.

"Eight this evening? Do you mean to tell me that you're prepared to drop everything right this minute and fly to England to bring Gray here?"

Jakub shrugged. "When Bracha died, I promised myself I'd never waste another moment," he said. "Time is so very precious."

At ten thirty the next morning, Father and I were interrupted at our game of gin rummy by a knock on the door of the suite. I jumped up from my seat, but Geoffrey, whose bedroom was closest to the entryway, got there first.

"A priest?" I heard him say as he opened the door in his dressing gown. "We don't need a priest." A split-second later, he recognized Gray. "Dear fellow, don't tell me you've become a papist!"

My brother entered the room, wearing a cassock. He looked as if he'd stepped out of some nineteenth-century religious pageant. Father was chuckling as he raised himself from the sofa. "So, have you come to hear my sins?" he said. "I've already confessed to Cara, although I suppose I could always confess a different set of sins to you. I have no shortage."

Gray reached him and the two of them hugged. "Father, it's so good to see you."

"Extraordinary!" Geoffrey was saying. "However did you come up with the idea of disguising yourself as a priest, dear boy?"

My brother was fumbling with the buttons of his cassock. "I

had nothing to do with the operation. It was presented to me last night as a *fait accompli*."

"Robbie?" Father shook his head. Geoffrey turned to me, eyebrows raised in disbelief.

"Here's the mastermind of the caper," I said with a laugh, rushing to Jakub, who was standing in the doorway, as if awaiting an invitation to come inside. I linked an arm through his and brought him over to sit with me next to Father on the sofa. Gray took an armchair across from us. Father asked Geoffrey to phone down for a bottle of champagne and while we waited for it to be delivered, Gray narrated the account of their escapade. The only dicey moment, it seems, was when a pair of nuns in the airport lobby tried to engage "the priest" in conversation over religious matters. Quick thinking on Jakub's part had saved the day. Pulling Claude's trusty Bible from his satchel, he read aloud from the Psalms while Gray bowed his head, giving himself over to devotion, until the flight was called.

"I almost converted to Catholicism on the spot," said Gray. "I tell you, he read with such fervor, I felt called to follow the path of righteousness."

When the champagne arrived, Father raised his glass to Jakub. "Here's to our miracle worker, Jakub Abramowicz."

"Hear, hear!" Geoffrey said, following suit. He drank off his glass in one swallow, then narrowed his eyes and scrutinized Jakub. "Are you certain you're a *Jewish* boy, dear fellow?"

"Quite certain," Jakub assured him. "But I also felt compelled to live up to the part when I wore the cassock."

He and Gray had apparently discussed a good many things in the time they'd spent together. Indeed, my brother had come to a momentous decision during the trip to Cannes. He'd made up his mind to return to the United States and face the consequences of his youthful indiscretions. I saw Geoffrey blanch when Gray told us that he was prepared to go before the

House Committee on Un-American Activities.

Gray also noticed Geoffrey's reaction. "I said I would appear. I didn't say I'd testify. I'll take the Fifth."

"You'll go to jail," Geoffrey countered. Nervously, he patted the pockets of his dressing gown, searching for cigarettes. "The Hollywood Ten were all sentenced, you know. Lardner and Trumbo served a year and their careers are finished now. Nobody will hire them."

Father interceded on Gray's behalf. "I'll find him work. I'll produce his play and if need be, I'll finance it myself, hock the lodge to raise the funds if the studios won't come through."

"Thank you, Father. I hope that won't be necessary, but it's a wonderful offer."

"I'm proud of you, son," Father said. "And Cara, that's quite a fine young man you've found yourself."

I turned and gave Jakub a kiss on the cheek, which caused him to blush endearingly.

Geoffrey was still flustered. "It isn't easy to stand up to those scoundrels, with their threats and insinuations. They know far more than you might think . . ."

"Unlike you, I never recruited for the Party," said Gray coldly. "And also unlike you, I would never name a single person I knew."

"Recruited, you say?" Father gave Geoffrey a sharp look. "Whom did you recruit?"

Abruptly, Geoffrey left the room. He returned, holding a pack of cigarettes. Shifting from one foot to the other, too agitated to sit down, he extracted a cigarette and lit it, inhaling deeply.

Father spoke in a quiet voice: "You recruited Vivien, didn't you?"

"That's preposterous!" said Geoffrey, indignantly exhaling. "Vivien would have made a terrible Party member. Anybody could see she lacked the commitment. It was all a game to her."

"Nevertheless, you did recruit her," Gray persisted. "She told me how you'd meet her in some dive out in South Central and take her to branch meetings."

Next to me on the sofa, I could feel Father trembling. "Is this true?"

"Yes, yes. I took her to a few meetings." Geoffrey was looking not at Gray, but at Father, laying out his case as if he were on trial. "You must understand, Robbie. It was Vivien's idea to join the Party. She was quite keen for it, but I must say, in retrospect, that it was an unwise thing, to have introduced her into those circles. She treated it like some spy film she was acting in, dressing in cheap clothes to disguise herself from the press, sneaking out for our secret rendezvous when we could just as easily have left the house together and driven there in her car." By this time, he was pacing, circling the room, pausing every now and then to draw on his cigarette. "I humored her. Yes, that's all I did. I humored her. And believe me when I say that I regret it deeply."

Something was nagging at me, but it was hard to isolate what it was. I sensed Jakub's distress at being made witness to a family drama, and a part of me wanted to run away and take him with me. I longed to reassure him; we'd spent almost no time together in private and here he was, caught up in old injuries, his great service to us all but forgotten. But of course there was Father to consider. His fragile health might not withstand the emotional impact of this new information. Reading the letters had precipitated one collapse, and I blamed myself for that already. Geoffrey's revelations threatened to provoke another crisis and I was anxious to end the conversation before that happened.

But I also worried about Gray and Geoffrey. If left alone, I feared they might come to blows. I felt pulled in so many directions, overwhelmed by responsibilities toward the people I loved, and yet there was something important that I needed to pay attention to, something flittering at the edge of my mind. Something about Vivien. A piece of the puzzle I'd been handed, the puzzle of her death. What was it? I probed my memory of my mother's final months, all that I'd learned from her letters, along with the details Father had filled in during our painful conversation.

Suddenly I knew: Geoffrey was the person my mother was meeting in secret, not Gray. The person the detective saw her with on multiple occasions, the "mysterious man" described by the tabloids. When Father confronted her with the evidence of her supposed infidelity, her first instinct would have been to deny the whole thing outright. It wasn't true, after all. But once he threw her out of the house and threatened to divorce her, to whom else could she have turned but to Geoffrey? In her nightgown, I could imagine her making her way across the grounds to his cabin. Crying, she would have told him that they'd been found out, their clandestine meetings discovered. And then wouldn't she have warned him that she was going to confess the truth to Father, to prevent him from carrying out his threat? And if she had done that, what would have happened to Geoffrey? It was wartime, and he was not only a pacifist, he was a Communist Party member and foreign-born, to boot. The government would have wasted no time in deporting him. Once back in England, he would have been thrown in jail. The Hindu pose was just a pose. I'd seen the true Geoffrey on the ship; he had expensive tastes, and no real interest in a Gandhi-esque self-sacrifice. What wouldn't he have done, to protect himself?

Horrified, I stood up. Geoffrey was standing near the balcony doors, surveying the four of us quite calmly. I took a step toward him, then another, and he backed up, as if trying to escape judgment.

"You killed my mother!"

I saw Geoffrey flick his cigarette away and reach into the pocket of his dressing gown. I kept moving toward him. I suppose I wanted to keep him in sight, expecting him to admit his guilt in front of us. I wasn't thinking clearly; although I'd just accused him of murder, I still didn't see him as dangerous. Behind me, the others began talking loudly, all at once.

"Geoffrey, is that a dueling pistol?" said Father.

Gray's voice, harsh: "Don't be a fool."

"Cara!" shouted Jakub. "Get down!"

I threw myself down on the carpet and ducked my head between my knees. Squeezing my eyes shut, I tried to make myself as small a target as possible. An instant later I heard a deafening explosion and the sound of breaking glass. A voice cried out in pain. Something heavy crashed to the floor. There were shouts and I felt someone rush past me.

"Be careful!" Gray exclaimed. "He's got another pistol!"

I opened my eyes and saw Gray tending to Father. Blood was flowing from several cuts on his face and head. The bullet had hit a lamp on the side table, and shattered glass was everywhere. Jakub was wrestling with Geoffrey not two feet from where I was crouched, gripping the arm that held the gun with both of his hands to prevent the Englishman from firing his weapon. The two of them slammed against the door frame and Geoffrey let out an oath as Jakub wrenched his arm back, releasing the pistol, which clattered to the floor. They both dived for it, but Geoffrey reached it first. He gave Jakub a savage kick, and scrambled to his feet. Gray was coming toward him now from the other direction, but Geoffrey was ready. I saw him point the gun at my brother and cock the trigger.

"No!" This time I didn't wait for him to fire, I just acted on instinct, launching myself at Geoffrey like a wild beast and knocking him to the ground. *The gun,* I was thinking, attempting to immobilize him with the weight of my own body. He was still grasping the pistol. I seized his arm and sunk my teeth into the flesh of his wrist, biting down hard until I felt his tendons loosen. Seizing the pistol, I struggled to my knees, placing the muzzle right up against Geoffrey's temple.

"If you move, I'll shoot!" My hand was trembling badly, but I must have sounded like I meant it, because he froze instantly.

Jakub came to kneel beside me and took the gun from my hand. "I'm here now. Call for help," he said. "Tell them to send an ambulance. And the police. Unless you'd like me to handle this now."

I shook my head no and got to my feet.

CHAPTER THIRTEEN:
WALDEN LODGE
SEPTEMBER 1956

Father's wounds were not serious, but it took time for him to heal, and we postponed our sailing for a month, to give me time to retrieve Fog from London and close up the little house in Hampstead. This delay also enabled us to provide evidence at Geoffrey's arraignment, and to plan for Gray's return to the United States. The French authorities were not the least bit interested in my brother's long-ago ties to international Communism; indeed, the magistrate had apparently been a member of the Communist Resistance. A few days after the hearing, a set of travel documents for Gray were delivered to the suite, allowing him to make the trip home under French protection.

Geoffrey's betrayal hit Father hard. He was no more able to forgive himself for the part he had played in Vivien's murder than when he'd blamed himself for her suicide. Not every moment of our time in Cannes was spent brooding over the past. With the festival over and summer not yet upon us, the Riviera was a delightful place to be. Luca and Francesca put off their return to Italy to spend time with us, and of course the actress was overjoyed to see her handsome "Gypsy" again.

"You see, Padre Pio had a plan for you as well, *carissima.*" It was fruitless to point out that I'd never made it to San Giovanni Rotondo. The good father had evidently discerned my heart's desire and answered my prayers, along with Francesca's—a double miracle that she and Luca would duly acknowledge by naming Jakub and me godparents of their son.

Jakub's trio was playing nearby. Juan-les-Pins was still a sleepy town in those days, but was already known as a Mecca for jazz lovers. One night, we all went to hear them, and during the second set I was persuaded to get up on stage with them and sing. I chose a Jerome Kern number for my debut, "All the Things You Are," and when I got to the final reprise, I turned to look at my beloved and sang the words to him and him alone. "You are the angel glow that lights a star," I began, but I never finished the stanza, for Jakub had put down his violin and taken me into his arms.

We always close our sets with "All the Things You Are." They played it at our wedding, which took place at the lodge in late September, once we knew for sure Gray wouldn't be going to prison. The Red Scare was dying down, and the activities of American Communists and fellow-travelers were not attracting the same outrage. He could have stayed in Hollywood, writing screenplays under his own name, but London had become his home.

As for Jakub and me, the world has become our home. Drifting from one gig to the next, never settling down in one place, might not suit everyone, but I figure we're just taking our cue from Khalil Gibran:

> "For that which is boundless in you abides in the
>   mansion of the sky,
> "whose door is the morning mist,
> "and whose windows are the songs and the
>   silences of night."

ABOUT THE AUTHOR

Lisa Lieberman is the author of numerous works of postwar European history and the founder of the classic movie blog Deathless Prose (*http://deathlessprose.com*). Trained as a modern European cultural and intellectual historian, she studied at the University of Pennsylvania and Yale University and taught for many years at Dickinson College. She now directs a nonprofit foundation dedicated to redressing racial and economic inequity in public elementary and secondary schools. In her spare time, she lectures on postwar efforts to come to terms with the trauma of the Holocaust in film and literature. After dragging their three children all over Europe while they were growing up, Lieberman and her husband are happily settled in Amherst, Massachusetts.